A Tapestry of Voices

Janet Browning

"Tapestry"

A Tapestry of Voices

An East Tennessee Anthology

Edited by
Kay Newton and Doris Ivie

A publication of the
Knoxville Writers' Guild
Knoxville, Tennessee

Copyright © 2011 by individual contributors
Copyright © 2011 by Knoxville Writers' Guild
A Tapestry of Voices: An East Tennessee Anthology
ISBN: 0-9643178-7-1

Printed in USA
by Lightning Source, Inc.

Knoxville Writers' Guild
P.O. Box 10326
Knoxville, Tennessee 37939-0326
http://www.knoxvillewritersguild.org

A Note on the Cover Art

For many in the Knoxville area, as well as other places throughout the country and the world, the name Cynthia Markert immediately conjures visions of the women she paints in oil on wood—haunting, mysterious women who convey a sense of sophistication shrouded in secrecy, women who have become so iconic that some refer to Cynthia as "the Modigliani of the New Millennium." Not everyone recognizes that she is also an accomplished photographer with a special knack for capturing the essence of local scenes, objects, landmarks, and landscapes. Photos from her two series "my knoxville" and "my maplehurst" appear on greeting cards alongside the ones portraying those familiar women and are just as distinctive and appealing in their own way.

Perched in her apartment on a hillside in Maplehurst, Cynthia has had—is having—the dubious pleasure of experiencing firsthand the deconstruction of the Henley Street Bridge, complete with all its dust, noise, and drama. She is producing a series of photographs of the process which will culminate in a show of its own after the project is complete. We are fortunate to have for our cover one of the photos from this series: a partially demolished arch of the bridge with the tower of Church Street Methodist Church in the background, a thoroughly urban mid-Knoxville scene somehow made splendidly bucolic by wispy white clouds floating in the robin's-egg blue sky seen through the arch. It's reassuring to know that long after the grand old bridge is demolished and reconstructed, its majesty will be preserved in Cynthia's art, and we're honored and privileged to have it on the cover of A Tapestry of Voices. Thank you, Cynthia.

Kay Newton, Editor

Table of Contents

Introduction

When I was first approached about taking the job of editing this anthology, I hesitated—not because I didn't know how to go about it (I didn't, but I've never let my ignorance get in the way of tackling a project), but because although I publish poetry only sparingly, I've had at least one piece in each of the previous KWG anthologies; and I knew I couldn't submit my own work to a publication I would be editing. That caveat was soon overcome: the prospect of having a significant role in producing a work in a literary series I admire and respect for its quality was too much to resist.

My first task was to choose an assistant editor. Immediately, I thought of my life-long friend, Dr. Doris Ivie, whose prior experience editing a KWG anthology (*Breathing the Same Air*) presumably meant she'd be able to guide me through the editorial process. In no time, her expertise, insight, and plain old hard work earned her a promotion from assistant to co-editor. Without her inestimable help this book would not be; she has my undying gratitude.

Before I came on board, the anthology committee had already chosen our theme: "diversity," in whatever way that term might be defined by each contributor. We think you'll find this eighth anthology fills that bill: the works here range in *genre* from song lyrics to a novel chapter; the stylistic forms vary from straightforward prose to free verse to an Italian sonnet; and the cast of characters includes, among others, a pastor who polishes his fingernails as a way of letting his parishioners know he empathizes with gays; a boy whose demented grandfather gives him the secret to finding love and happiness; and a palace guard charged with overseeing the execution of a Syrian ruler, to name but a few. The geographical settings of these works may vary from Greece to

Mexico to France and elsewhere, but all the writers have in common a connection to East Tennessee; so it's not surprising that many of the works are set right here.

Interspersed among the written pieces are graphics: drawings, paintings, and photographs that represent the widely varied talents of our contributors, some of whom have both literary and visual art in this volume. From Cynthia Markert's cover photograph of the Henley Street Bridge deconstruction to a painting of hands on the fretboard of a stringed instrument, the artwork enhances and reinforces the written material here.

By turns, this book may make you laugh; it may make you cry; but above all, it will make you appreciate the diverse voices woven into the unique tapestry comprising the East Tennessee literary and artistic community. We hope you enjoy it.

Kay Newton, Editor

The Knoxville Writers' Guild continues to breathe life into a part of my being that I often ignore, and for that gift I remain grateful. Linda Parsons Marion and Candance Reaves prompted me to submit some of my poetry for the second KWG anthology, *All Around Us: Poems from the Valley*, in which they published three of my poems. I was hooked. I began writing again. I joined the Guild.

Before I knew it, Candee had encouraged me to serve on the KWG Board, and after having assisted numerous elders in crafting their memoirs for *The Voice of Memory: A Collection of Memoirs*, I found myself agreeing to edit *Breathing the Same Air: An East Tennessee Anthology* (Celtic Cat Publishing, 2001). While sometimes spending over a hundred hours a week working on that anthology during summer 2000, I swore I'd never again undertake such a task.

And then, a decade later, my long-time friend Kay Newton, with whom I shared an office in the UTK English Department forty years ago, invited me to help her birth the feisty anthology you are now holding. I protested, "No way!" and rattled off myriad reasons not to tie up another year of my life with an anthology project. But the opportunity to work so closely with Kay ultimately proved too enticing to resist, as was the opportunity to help empower writers from often-ignored communities by including their works alongside those of "established writers" in this anthology. Besides, this time there was an enthusiastic, active anthology committee who had already written grant proposals and who later assisted us in selecting the works published herein.

Kay offered her elegant, yet divinely comfortable, restored Victorian home for our work sessions and generously shared the companionship of her one-eyed pug Popeye and her most recent clutch of cats. Each time we worked together I felt transported, luxuriating in a world that only Kay Newton could create and inhabit so graciously.

I think of myself as one of the few remaining nitpicky editors on the planet (I am appalled by the errors that appear in today's newspapers and even in some literary magazines), but Kay matched me nit for nit as we groomed, honed and polished many of the works herein. We made the kinds of decisions about consistency that editors must make, and along the way, we learned that some usages once labeled "nonstandard" or even "illiteracies" were now (egads!) considered acceptable. Editors must not only stay abreast of change; they must also accept that "error gremlins" will work their ugly magic no matter how scrupulous we have been. Should you find errors herein, tip your hat to those unseen forces that challenge and conquer perfectionism.

Kay has ably introduced you to the contents of this compilation, so I'll just say I am now grateful that I once again said "yes" to participate in such a labor of love, and that I hope each of you will get as involved in the Guild's work as Kay and I have over the years. The rewards of Guild membership and Guild service are as surprisingly varied—and sometimes as delightful—as the contents of this book. But for now, kick back and marvel with us at this "tapestry of voices."

Doris Ivie, Editor

Acknowledgments

We would like to express our sincere appreciation to all those who have had any part in bringing this book about.

Our thanks go to the Tennessee Arts Commission for their generous grant.

TENNESSEE ARTS COMMISSION

The Anthology Committee also has our gratitude:

> Martha Yarnell, Chair
> Meg Bensey
> Carole Ann Borges
> Judith L. Duvall
> Cathy Kodra
> Kim R. West

Special thanks also go to Kim R. West for her design of this anthology.

We are indebted to Jeff Gordon and Kelly Norrell for their help with publicity.

Our contributors deserve the lion's share of credit for the creation of this book.

Thanks also go to the Guild Board and to the general membership for their support and encouragement.

Photograph on preceding page:

Melanie Harless

"The Search for Enlightenment"

Lucy Sieger

A Greater Mosaic

I'm afflicted with spiritual polygamy. I've kept Easter Vigil with the Episcopalians, sat in sun-drenched silence with the Quakers, chanted vibrating Oms with the Hindus, meditated with a Zen priestess, and caroled with the Methodists. One Friday night, at a Jewish temple, I embraced a Shabbat I would not keep.

A few years ago, I began visiting a progressive Catholic Church, John XXIII, on a university campus near my home. For a while, every Mass made me cry, unobtrusively and gently, like a rainy reunion. My family's long Catholic heritage was diluted by the time I grew up in the '70s, so perhaps I was channeling my great-grandmothers' tears of joy that I was back in the fold. Despite profound, painful differences with the Vatican, differences shared by many fellow parishioners, I settled into an uneasy, compartmentalized worship. Being a liberal Catholic woman meant compromising political principles for sustenance of the soul.

Not surprisingly, I've been wandering again, occasionally skipping Mass for stealth forays to other ecclesiastical pastures. One Sunday, I attended a service at the local Unitarian Universalist church. The music was rousing, the sermon provocative, but I grew frustrated as we praised "the weaver of our lives." This coy higher power dissatisfied me. I craved God, a loving, personal God, a politically correct version of the tangible Holy Spirit that infused me at John XXIII.

The following Tuesday, I taught the gospel lesson at our weekly class for incoming Catholics. As we discussed Jesus luring Peter and Andrew away from their fishing nets, I wondered if anyone could tell I had strayed. Was I the unwitting bearer of a theological hickey?

It wouldn't be the first time. I belonged to a small ministry group of six Catholics, mostly ornery Catholics of liberal bent, who had returned to the church after years away. Our meetings revolved around food and wine – Catholics love wine. After all, it's a sacrament. At one dinner party, in a blush of honest faith-sharing, I asked, "Okay, do you all *really* believe that Jesus was literally raised from the dead? Or is the resurrection a metaphor for redemption?" To a person, they answered: Jesus died for our sins, was raised from the dead, and sits at the right hand of the Father. No doubts. I was not condemned for the question, but the pity in their voices stung.

I accept the resurrection of Jesus as the cornerstone of Christianity. But accepting a tenet out of obedience and deeply believing it are two different constructs. I consider the scripture verse I whisper when facing a daunting task: I can do all things through Christ who strengthens me (Philippians 4:13). This precious mantra always calms me, always empowers me. If Christ is in each of us, then perhaps his energy is manifested in my most courageous self. I can grasp that sort of theology for a few seconds, before it twists into a pretzel of rationalist doubt. Is it Christ, or my belief in Christ, that gives me strength?

At times, I spend too much time pondering this, and my head throbs. I know and love many good people who live decent, even divine lives without needing a religion to codify them. They don't devour books and scour the Internet looking for clues as to who Jesus was and was not; they don't hunt for the perfect theology that heals every gaping crevice in their psyches.

As it happens, I'm married to such a contented spirit. While I navigate another unfamiliar pew on another Sunday morning, Mark worships at the park down the street, ambling with our dogs along a luminous trail bordering an oblique river. He wouldn't frame it this way, but his religion is as simple as being present. I wish I could attain so much, and be satisfied with so little.

Instead, I try to know God, which is a slippery concept, like infinity. My mortal brain cannot conceive of a universe with no end, but my spirit soars at the possibility. In a moment of clarity, I realize that infinity lets me off the hook. If I'm inspired by the absence of cosmic boundaries, why search for the perfect doctrinal fence to restrain me? Why subject my own ideology to a constricted hypothesis if the expansive dimensions of the heavens themselves are inexplicable? Why not allow my faith, my powerful yearning for palpable yet unseen transcendence, this same roaming freedom and consummate mystery?

I've been living a Zen koan. I may worship at a Catholic church, yet I'm more than one faith, and not fully any faith. In the eyes of organized religion, I will always be a theological misfit, but I have the world's abundant spiritual wisdom as solace. As fervently as my Catholic friends believe in the literal resurrection of Jesus, I believe that my fragmented soul is part of a greater mosaic. This mosaic spans creeds and cultures and planets and time, and will fascinate me until my last breath.

Valentino Constantinou

"Pebbles"

Clyde Croswell

Mindfulness

"Imagination is more important than knowledge" – Einstein

When time is taken and
routine thought and habit arrested,
art and imagination merge.

Like pickaxe work tending hardened ground,
ego falls away. Like an eagle's molting,
a serpent shedding its old tired skin,
a novel self emerges, hospice worker
for the old, midwife for the new.

We become participating observers,
infinite potential, transforming space and
matter, time and eternity, pure energy set free.

More source than outcome, more art
than science, beyond the biases
of modernity or mere computation, the rare
and precious sacred mind of contemplation.

Kim R. West
"Odd Friends"

Judith L. Duvall

City Friends

An unlikely pair, goose and crow:
one swoops low, one waddles
summer-hot pavement, picks
at sparse grass, seeks safety
from city trucks, loaded vans.

Feathered communication
thought awkward across species
defies science, finds comfort
in a unified search and seize,
companioned squawk and caw.

Beyond bare concrete's unforgiving
borders, a secret of sorts,
the unexpected cool of an ancient creek
briar-covered, safe from missiles
aimed by roving boys.

A freight train's endless complaint
thunders through the crossing.
Goose, a statue in black and gray,
waits for quiet to return.
Crow spirals high, caws warnings.

At evening pause, goose soaks tired
feet in a tepid, oily puddle;
loyal crow, fierce guardian
of friendship formed,
murmurs night-watch sounds from her perch.

Margo Miller

"Pecking Order"

Robert L. Beasley

The Rector Painted His Nails

Little Julia lifted her hand to catch his eye. Caught, he knew what he would do.

She knelt at the altar rail on Pentecost Sunday. Like most everybody, she was decked in red. She didn't make the usual cross with her hands to receive the Body of Christ. As she extended her right palm, Father Joseph Grumman placed the bread there. She raised and gently curved her left hand to show him her nails. Vermillion, maroon, magenta, fuchsia, and one pink with a white stripe. A seven-year-old, she beamed, proud to be a painted lady. And, though captured in a pleasing tent of transfiguration with Julia, with a glory like being on the holy mount with Jesus, Moses, and Elijah, he moved down the mountain to give communion to Sylvia, a taciturn, righteous woman, a big red Medusa kneeling next to little Julia. The road down the mountain eventually turns upward to the hill of Calvary.

That evening he painted his nails. First, he slept. He had to more than ever now. Sunday morning seemed longer and more rigorous. He craved Sunday afternoon solitude, but when he awoke, his sleep had been too much, too deep.

He puttered around and fixed some tea, watched a little news, and finally settled on Emma's photo. What form had she become? The seed, the emerging spiritual body? Joe's vision faltered. He hummed a few bars from "Alleluia, Sing to Jesus." Her favorite, so they had sung it with tear-quenching vigor at the funeral. He turned the line about the crystal sea over in his heart. And it just seemed like enough, enough of that; something had to happen.

Joseph Grumman opened Emma's makeup drawer, sealed like a tomb since that dark day in Advent. He chose the lavender. He'd always wanted to wear the bishop's purple. No bishop's ring but, damn, his fingernails looked regal.

The red Medusa came to the office for her regular admin meeting the next morning. God and St. Anne's congregation elected Sylvia Winterholt as the Senior Warden, the top layperson, his closest confidante, the director of temporal affairs. Or so she reminded Father Joe as often as possible. This year he needed a lot of reminding. Death distracts the good order of life.

Moreover, the backlash to the election of the gay bishop prompted Sylvia's election. Father Joe's obvious support of the new bishop complicated matters. So Sylvia scored one for propriety during their first meeting. "Some very good people think you're too accepting of moral degeneration. You can love those people, and we all do, but we can't lose all our standards." Failing her became a weekly ritual.

Today, she talked about the money people withheld, but her eyes followed his hands. He touched his chin. She stared. He put his hands in his lap. She stared. He gestured to the leak in the corner of the ceiling. She stared. Finally, she said, "Father, is something wrong with your nails?"

"No, they're fine."

"But . . . they're painted, aren't they? Maybe a fungus or something?"

"No, they're just polished. You know, nail polish."

The look. Worth a prized possession. He wondered if he had ever known in his fifty-nine years what dumbfounded meant.

It didn't take long for the red Medusa to spread the news about Father Joe's manicure throughout the parish.

That evening the phone rang as he opened the door. Two quick strides and he caught it. "Joe, it's Roland, I'm on my way to Tuckaway Cove for the Provincial Bishop's meeting. How are you doing?"

"Good, very good," Joe replied, but knowing the busy bishop didn't call to check his health.

"Listen, Joe, Madge at the office has been on the phone about three times today with Sylvia Winterholt. I'm between planes here. Madge doesn't use the word hysterical much. What's this about your nails?"

"Nothing much, Bishop, they're just a beautiful lavender right now."

"You really painted them? A color?"

"I did."

"Joe, are you all right? I know things have been hard since Emma died. I should have seen you more, I guess."

"I'm fine; I'm working through that okay."

"Well, this is really strange behavior, Joe. Don't you think? I mean painting your nails and all."

Joe let some silence slip in, then said, "Well, I've been thinking, Bishop, and somehow I feel that I just might be gay."

The Bishop let some silence slip in and then said, "Joe, you know I'm gonna support you, but slow down. Don't talk to anybody about this yet. I'll be back next Tuesday and we'll have a sit-down. I've got to board this plane now. Just take it easy. Okay?"

"I am taking it easy and I will do an even better job of that now."

"And Joe?"

"Yes."

"You might want to clean that stuff off those nails for now."

What a whirlwind surrounded him Tuesday. Stella, the parish secretary, bounced from one phone call to the next, falling ever more behind on mailing the newsletter. Not that anyone called to ask if he had painted his nails. Just checking to see how things were going.

The Women's Luncheon rose from its doldrums. To Sylvia's horror several women crowded around to inspect his hands. Sue Carpenter even gave him some tips on keeping the polish on the nail. Joan Freeman suggested he clean it all off, get a professional manicure, and do it right.

He stood before the women for a program on friendship. Like many of them he had lost his best friend, so they commiserated a little. He drew out the friendship of David and Jonathan and then of Jesus and the Beloved Disciple. At the close, they sang "What a Friend We Have in Jesus."

Late in the afternoon, Sylvia caught him on his cell. "We're calling a meeting."

"We?"

"The Vestry."

"I thought I called the meetings."

"Well, of course you do, so you're calling this one. We'll meet at my house and I hope you'll be there."

To go or not to go: that is the question. But why not? He bought this ticket anyway.

Sylvia's husband George greeted him at the door. He extended a warm hand of welcome while his eyes glanced downward. Sylvia darted close behind, taking Joe's arm and ushering him into the downstairs rec room. Though Joe arrived on time, somehow he descended the stairs last. Like Dante's purgatory, except in reverse. Only ten of the twelve members were scattered about the room, along with George, all with wine, a half-eaten cheese plate on the table by the sofa. Sylvia offered him a glass and bid everyone to sit. She took the place to his right. "Father, maybe you could open with a prayer and call us to order."

He did so, then said, "Well, I suppose the business at hand is my nails."

Sylvia jumped in. "Not exactly, Father Joe. We want first to say how much we respect you and are concerned for you." She lifted and spread her arms as if to plead for divine intervention. "We know St. Anne's has been hurting, and we know you have been, especially since Emma died. We want to help you along and help our beloved church."

Joe looked around the room at the nods that accompanied her soliloquy. The time had come. "So it's not about my nails? You're okay with my nails?"

"It's like they're a symptom, Father. Maybe things aren't feeling the way you'd like them to and you did this thing . . . for whatever reason. We want to help you." She motioned around the circle of Vestry members then raised her voice a decibel and spoke more quickly. "But, we don't know how to explain this to our friends. People are laughing at St. Anne's. It's been hard enough with all this gay stuff. Now you're . . . well, you're doing whatever you're doing."

"I think I could be gay."

Sylvia leaned far away, spread her eyelids, and shook her head in a slow bewildered motion. "I guess it had to be. You wouldn't be so in favor of them if you hadn't fallen under their spell." She looked at the floor. "I hope you haven't done anything to really embarrass us."

Husband George stared at Joe from across the room. His eyes remained steady, face unruffled. "Do you have a partner, Joe?"

"Oh no, nothing like that."

"I'm sorry to ask, a lover maybe?"

"Heavens, no."

Sylvia squinted her eyes and leaned back toward him. "Well, have you been with some guy?"

"No, I haven't."

"Well, shit, Father!" She slapped her thigh. "How do you know you're gay? You were married to Emma for thirty-five years. You fathered three children. How can you suddenly be gay?"

"Well, I'm all alone. They've been such nice people since I spoke up for them. I think I'm one of them. Solidarity, you know."

"Father Joe! You've lost . . . I can't . . . ."

She paused just enough for George to speak. "Sylvia, let me, please, ask Father this. So you haven't consummated any relationship which, as Sylvia feels, might embarrass the church?"

"That's right; I haven't. . . . Yet."

Others began to talk among themselves: If you weren't doing it and never had, were you, or not? Couldn't be. Yeah, you could, 'cause it's in your blood. But someone could be oriented but not really be one. Stephen, a banker, whose family had long standing in the parish, asked, "Isn't it okay? I mean, hasn't the church said it's okay to be oriented?"

Bert, the concrete dealer, asked, "So the nails, I mean, it's kind of like one of my guys wearing an earring or something, right?"

"I just wanted to do it. I've turned a corner. Maybe wanted you to read the directions."

Sylvia tried to bring the meeting to order. "We still have to decide something about this and our church. I can't abide the bad image we have. We need to ask the Bishop to relieve Father Joe of his duties, and I so move." A spirited debate followed. Much of it about Joe in front of Joe. In the end the motion failed seven to three.

George accompanied Joe to the door. Shaking Joe's hand, he said, "Not bad, Joe, point well made. Seems like I heard once about people in Holland all wearing a star of David during the German occupation. Solidarity like that?"

Joe smiled a little. "Might even make the world a better place. What a thought, George."

Sunday became an interesting day. Joe couldn't say it bubbled with joy but the tone was far from dull. People stepped about with more liveliness in their strides; clusters of little conversations took place on the steps outside and in the entry to the church. Except for Sylvia. She looked like she forgot her makeup. The good news: she came. With George scheduled to read a lesson in worship, maybe she thought she had to. But at least she was present and accounted for.

Before Sunday School little Julia had found him in the hallway and asked to see his nails. Her little hands spread his fingers and drank in the sight. She said they looked good, but maybe he should try stripes or something.

The Gospel reading told of the disciples plucking grain on the Sabbath. He told them he couldn't preach on the goodness of lawbreaking. However, he was stretching the rules for the good of others – that they might go and do. The communion produced a warmth in the air and under the skin. While serving the Host, he almost cried when he noticed Stephen's son extending a hand with one thumbnail painted.

William Isom II

Appalachian Mulatto

The wind blows whiffs
Of continued struggle,
Our atmosphere thickly smoked spliffs.
Can I explain how grungy,
Dirty, dark and muggy
This South really is?
Bands of us roam this ground
Rooted in that Lost and Found
Kudzu covers and smothers.
Swimming in greenery so lush
This is where we take our
Mired stands,
Abandoned plants,
Unemployed, drunken
Backstrokers
Bloodshot-eyed tokers.
Skin palettes mingle
Long-sleeved Mexican
Slave-trade (you'd-better-be-bilingual)
Sticky characters misplaced,
At home un-united, but here
The loyalty backbones their hate.
We grow, continually live—
Poison ivy, contagious,
Spreading beautiful hues;
Children and neighbors reveal
Those dark, melanin clues.
Crisp, dry labels have

Been cleanly applied
While centuries we hide.
Methodically mixing
Like a mad scientist's brew
Bubbling various DNA,
The labels remain, irremovable glue.
Our Nation has yet
To rank and file,
Parade and flag wave,
And . . . I don't think that we would
Save, saving, *saved*
For what's to come.
Black-minded
One-Drop Rule and such,
Cultures broiled into mush,
A new brew.
Stewed ideology
We can't stand that
Pure, claimed lineage
And stay marginalized until
Surprise, surprise, surprise!
Babies with red clay to the bone
Manifest in what your daughter brings home.

Jeannette Brown

Proper Nouns

Cherokees, poets, and pioneers
called things into being with
names—Round Bottom,
Cat's Pajamas, Hangover Creek,
Hen Wallow and Coon Den.

Each stream, flower, bend,
falls, gap and boulder was called,
a song of the heart
its own poem describing its
place to the scudding clouds above.

Convergence of myth and botany,
Indian cry and goose call:
Place of a Thousand Drips
where the Sweet Heifer stands
under a Thunderhead.

Then came the one-note Scottish botanist
who walked through these woods
naming things after himself:
Fraser Fir, Fraser Sedge,
Fraser Magnolia.

Amy Staffaroni

"First Knoxville Winter"

John C. Mannone

Tanasi

> Eventually, all things merge into one, and a river runs
> through it. The river was cut by the world's great flood and
> runs over rocks from the basement of time. On some of the
> rocks are timeless raindrops. Under the rocks are the words,
> and some of the words are theirs. I am haunted by waters.
> — Norman McClean, A River Runs Through It

The Cherokee had a way with words.
Before their nation became the State
of Tennessee, they called it Tanasi,
the place where the river bends,
where the green water meets itself.
From the foothills of the Smoky Mountains,
the Cherokee, the Creek and the Yuchi
could see the confluence of rivers —
the Holston and the French Broad
that gave birth to the Tennessee —
And so could the German, French and Irish,
and the English, too.
Each in their own language spilled words
as blood, which would wash through
the ages into the Tennessee. Today,
I hear their whispers in the dogwoods,
their honeysuckle prayers, the swish of voices:
Sequoyah, Boudinot, John Ross.
When I breathe their names, I hear echoes
of generations hovering over waters,
their swollen fingers reaching out
over the great expanse of the valley.
These people who fashioned this land,
their tears still flow into the Tennessee.
Some have evaporated to heaven, yet fallen
again refreshing the land, but some left a trail.
I am silent. I sit on the bank and listen
to my own heartbeat measure that silence,
to the flow of the river over rocks, to the sound
of words there. To the sound of many waters,
the voices of nations.

Shannon Jones

"Untitled"

Ronnie James Vadala

Neddy Mountain

First Verse

G   C

Went up to Neddy Mountain from the valley down below

D7   G

I watched the French Broad River glisten brightly as it flowed

G   C

I saw the black bear and the deer, the cougar, and the owl

D7   C D7 G

And overhead an eagle flew, for he was on the prowl

Second Verse

G   C

I tried to understand his calls, and listened to his sounds

 D7   G

The eagle spoke about such beauty as I looked all around

G   C

The sycamores, and mountain streams, the flowers growing wild

D7   C D7 G

Not only there for me to see, but for tomorrow's child.

Chorus

 G   *Em* *Am*

The eagle said, take care, my friend, but tell your fellow man

 D7   *C*   *G*

Replace the gifts you take away from this our sacred land

 G   *Em* *Am*

This mountain is a home to me and the creatures left that roam

D7   C   G
It will not last forever if you strip away the gold
   G   Em   Am
One time there were such treasures that your eyes could not behold
   D7   C   G
When Neddy Mountain stood so tall and proud in the days of old.

Third Verse [CAPO Key Change]
G   C
Well I saw an Indian burial ground in a hollow by those hills
D7   G
When I heard a she-wolf howling there, the sound gave me the chills
   G   C
I traversed very lightly, and with great respect I prayed
D7   C   D7   G
The warriors that had roamed the land, now at peace they lay

Fourth Verse
G   C
The carvings on the stones that marked the graves a story told
D7   G
Of how the Cherokee Nation lived and hunted long ago
G   C
Until the white man's army there killed all the buffalo
D7   C   D7   G
Forced the Indians to the west, with nowhere else to go.

Chorus

```
     G         Em        Am
The eagle said, take care, my friend, but tell your fellow man
     D7                  C         G
Replace the gifts you take away from this our sacred land
     G         Em        Am
This mountain is a home to me and the creatures left that roam
     D7                  C         G
It will not last forever if you strip away the gold
     G         Em        Am
One time there were such treasures that your eyes could not behold
     D7                  C         G
When Neddy Mountain stood so tall and proud  in the  days of old.
```

Dick Penner

Silence

the slow sound of rain
on the roof each time I awake
then rushing winds
clacking the bamboo chimes
in the night's silence

Connie Jordan Green

Living with Snakes

My mother had nightmares about them,
couldn't look at a picture
of the great coiled body, tongue
like a finger beckoning. She told
how when she was young a neighbor boy
threw a dead snake on her, smooth body
wrapping her neck until she felt its spirit cut
her breath, fear drawing the constrictor close.

My dad kept one in his garden,
long, slender, black, quiet
beneath squash leaves, slipping
across his feet when he bent
to stroke it. Catcher of mice,
moles, whatever would eat
his crops before we could—leave
it alone, he told us girls.

I have come to need them,
watch them in the woodpile
where chipmunks spend the summer,
spot one on the basement stairs,
shut the door against my husband's discovery,
dark secret for my eyes only.

Judy Lockhart DiGregorio

Muddying Up the Gene Pool

"I don't believe in interracial marriage," read the first line of the handwritten letter from my father. It hadn't occurred to me that my father would interpret my engagement to an Italian-American quite that way.

I passed the letter on to my fiancé Dan sitting on a worn leather sofa in the dormitory common room. He reacted with astonishment.

"What's your father talking about? My skin's the same color as his."

I shook my head in frustration. My Scotch-Irish father grew up in the Hill Country of Texas in an isolated and impoverished community as tough as the Texas live oaks that thrived there. Dad's family taught him to view anyone with suspicion who was not white, Protestant, or a native of the Hill Country. This did not mean his family treated outsiders uncharitably. They never failed to help those in need, but they did not socialize with them. Dad's family was composed of people who were basically good but also ignorant about Jews, Catholics, Hispanics, and, I now realized, Italians.

"My Dad probably thinks you have a thick head of black hair and swarthy skin."

"Maybe he thinks I wear wife-beater T-shirts and stink of garlic breath."

"Probably."

"Well, I do like garlic," Dan said.

"And you definitely look Italian with that Roman nose. Not that it's unattractive." The situation would have been funny if it hadn't been so serious.

Dan and I were college juniors. It was naïve of me to announce my engagement by mail before my folks had even had the opportunity to meet him. But I was twenty years old, and I knew everything. Since our university was 300 miles away from my home in Capitan, N.M., and I had no car, I didn't visit home very often. And I couldn't easily phone my folks because in the small town where they lived, few people had a home phone. They were too expensive. Everyone used the one pay phone in town to make long distance calls.

Though Dan had not met my family, I had visited his a few months earlier in Gallup, N.M., when we rode home with one of Dan's friends. We were not engaged at that point, but his parents were very kind to me, plying me with tasty homemade pasta. His father could not wait to show me the barrels of fermenting zinfandel-grape wine he had made and stored in the basement. One sip of the fragrant wine, and I felt my knees grow weak. It was good, and it was strong.

When Dan proposed to me a month or so after the visit, I immediately said "yes." Wrapped in a cocoon of self-absorption, I didn't even think about discussing this important decision with my folks first. After Dan read Dad's comment on interracial marriage, he confessed that his mother wasn't thrilled about me either.

"What," I cried. "She doesn't like me?"

"It's not you," Dan replied." It's where you're from. Texas. She hates Texans."

"But why?"

"No reason. Just one of the prejudices she developed after she immigrated to the U.S. It doesn't make any more sense than your father's prejudice about Italians. People don't like what they don't know."

"She probably watched too many Westerns and decided all Texans are wild cowboys who carry guns and shoot up things," I concluded.

Dan's mother did have a point about some Texans. My father's side of the family included hard-working and hard-drinking ranchers who raised angora goats and cattle. Most of them did carry guns, but they used them for hunting deer, rabbits, or wild hogs. Some of my father's cousins acted pretty rambunctious at times. It was rumored that a couple of them once consumed so much beer at the annual Oktoberfest in New Braunfels, Texas, they started dancing on the tables in their boots and had to be forcibly removed from the festival.

After my parents finally met Dan in person, they were embarrassed by what my dad had written and tried hard to make him feel welcome. Dan's family also forgave me for having been born in the Lone Star State. Our wedding was a joyful and loud celebration with Dan's father serving homemade wine to cement the friendship between the pistol-toting Texans and the garlic-loving Italians.

Years later, Mom confessed that her own German-American family in Texas was horrified when they heard about Dad for the first time. Strict Methodists, they did not believe in drinking or dancing. And they weren't happy that Dad took Mom to Gruene Dance Hall where they served beer and danced the two-step. In addition, Dad was a former cowboy, even though he was making a living by driving a city bus in San Antonio at the time.

All of Mom's extended family, including her siblings and cousins, spoke German and English. They were uneasy about accepting someone who couldn't converse in both languages, and of course my father couldn't.

"He won't like German food, especially Koch Kase (a strong-smelling cheese)," they warned her.

And what kind of name was Lockhart, they asked? They preferred sturdy German names like Vordenbaumen, Sassmanhausen, or Rittiman.

My dad's easy-going temperament and strong work ethic finally won them over. Mom and Dad married in 1940. When he left for World War II, all of Mom's relatives proudly showed up to see him off.

Over the years, my parents had five children. As we married and created our own families, the make-up of the family changed. We added several Catholics, which worried Dad. He was sure the Pope would be running our lives from then on. However, the Pope never even noticed us.

Then one of my brothers married a lovely Hispanic girl. Dad raised his eyebrows at this but eventually adjusted and grew to enjoy the new family custom of eating spicy homemade tamales each Christmas. In due course, our family included adopted children and grandchildren, adding even more diversity to the gene pool.

We were bombarded with more diversity than we anticipated when my twenty-three year old daughter and her African-American boyfriend announced they were expecting a child. Surprise, anxiety, and fear consumed us as we came to terms with our own prejudices. With patience and understanding from all, we eventually navigated through the crisis. Our grandson arrived on a dewy May morning. One look at the coffee-colored bundle of joy with the luminous brown eyes, and we were smitten. A new chapter in our lives began that day, one that has brought us more delight than we ever anticipated.

Our family has changed considerably in the past years, and my 91-year-old father has mellowed like a fine Chardonnay since his conservative childhood in the Hill Country. His relatives now include people of different races, religions, and political outlooks. Like a blend of bold-flavored coffees, the gene pool has grown richer and stronger. Dad and the rest of us have learned to accept the challenge of diversity and embrace it. We now realize family is not a matter of having the right genes; it's a matter of having the right heart.

Janet Browning

"Just Married"

Jane Sasser

Cynthia

Stoop-shouldered, you stare up
at someone's camera, your white hair
a scant knot at your nape:
too stingy even to grow much hair.
The bony hands in your lap
never held your eleven babies
very tight—too busy trying
to put up jars of green beans,
to plow even the fields—
your father had no sons,
so you learned labor,
held it close
like the shape note hymns
you sang a cappella Sunday mornings
because pianos were a sin.
I don't want to claim you,
fierce woman who idolized
her sons, punished her daughters
with words like steel blades.
Don't look up, seventy-five and bent,
with watery, sad eyes—I don't want
to remember how, nineteen,
you ran off, down the road
to meet my grandfather,
wearing your Sunday-best slip
and a heart beating hope.

Patricia A. Hope

Meet Me in January

Meet me in January
near the backyard swing,
when the air is thin and each
breath we take goes before us.
Snuggle into the warmth of wool
like a lamb sheltered by its mother.

Pull your cap low over protruding ears,
push gloves snug around fingers.
Step into fur-lined boots and slough
across dead leaves and frozen ground.
Fill the bird feeders, check on the dogs,
make sure the horse trough isn't frozen over.

Feel the first sunlight on your face
as you spread hay for the cattle
Think about biscuits dripping with
butter and honey, sausage patties
and country ham, perfect eggs
still warm from the nest as I crack them
into my grandmother's skillet.

Hum a song of thanksgiving,
whisper an ode to those who cared
for this place before us.
Feel their spirit in the cold crisp morning,
swaying in the trees, hiding in the grass,
or sitting along the fence row
where momma deer feeds on the gooseberries.

Know you are honored among men
for you were given the life of the farmer,
protector of earth's fertility,
keeper of all that nourishes and sustains us.

Meet me in January when the air is thin
and we will pretend
we are farmers
barnstormers
mountain hikers
long-distance bikers
Anything . . . far from this city.

Richard P. Remine
 "Buck Dancing"

Marianne Worthington

Tennessee Barn Dance:
Little Darlin's Not My Name

It's not cousin, gal, honey or sweetheart.
Not little miss, little maid, little jo,
little shoe, little sunbonnet. Our names
aren't sister, girl, lady or aunt. Listen.
We had to play like one of the boys—cards,
drinking, jokes—to hold our own on radio,
at whistlestops, barn dances, school houses,
church meetings and every blazing county
fair in all the states they used for our names:
Montana, Louisiana, Texas.

Don't call us bluebird, songbird, nightingale,
cricket. Not sunshine, moonshine, violet
or sugar. Not brown eyes, black-eyed susie,
violet or laughin' lindy. If you want
us, holler the names our mothers gave us.
Recollect how we really were: raw-boned,
ready, pioneer, headliner, legend.
Does any of that sound little to you?

Penny L. Wallace
"String Dreams"

Jennifer Alldredge

Tarantella

Bradley blinked watery black eyes as he gazed at the shiny swirling skirts, silver and blue. They spun like a toy he would have remembered had he tried, but trying hurt. His toes wriggled inside ancient sneakers, and the distracting tip of one emerged, black and grey with old mud. Had he been down by the river again? The dark pools called to him, their soft depths promising to take away all he no longer wanted to remember.

A man with short pale hair joined the dancers and Bradley stepped back toward the low wrought-iron fence separating restaurant patrons from the rest of the people watching the outdoor performances on the square. The aromas of bacon and cinnamon wafted in a dance of their own, making his stomach rumble. The short-haired dancer frightened him; that kind of hair often wore a dark blue hat and uniform. Bradley wanted to leave before strong hands put him in some tiny room with others who understood only loudness and pain. Bradley knew about pain. He preferred the easily understood sharpness in the night when they thought you were hiding something. The other kind of pain created inside tears without relief. But the music called. So he closed his eyes, limbs twitching and shuddering with the sound and invisible images, and he let the world disappear.

~

"Oh, I love this part." Sarah put down her fork as the dancers gracefully executed a flawless twirl. "The Tarantella. The spider dance."

"That's tarantula, sweetie," Bonnie cooed. "The Tarantella is just some Italian dance." The other girls at the table snickered, early evening sunlight glinting off sparkling fingers as they lifted pink-stained glasses to carefully applied lips.

Sarah looked at her salad. "Actually, I read that it started in a town called Taranto and is about spiders. Something about if you're bitten by a tarantula you can dance all the poison out." The girls *oh reallied* appropriately as Sarah looked directly at Bonnie's eyes. "You just have to give in to the dance."

Bonnie carefully cut a sliver of rare meat, juices dripping as she lifted her fork. "Well," she said, "aren't you quite the fount of knowledge." Her white teeth turned momentarily red as she ate. Sarah felt an inexplicable inward victory and smiled down at her plate.

"So, not to change the subject, but have you all heard the latest about Sue's Married Mystery Lover?" Bonnie's silvery voice poured out as she lifted a wine bottle, shifting the bottle's neck to her glass, crimson liquid splashing tiny darts onto the snowy cloth.

Sarah stared at a drop as it spread a minuscule web, thin white threads absorbing the blush. She raised a hand to her face, patting her carefully coiffed hair into place to cover the heat rising in her cheeks. The others murmured their ignorance as Bonnie raised her glass.

"I hear that his wife suspects. Apparently he's backpedalling rapidly to cover his trail and showering the poor ignorant woman with expensive gifts to keep her in the dark." More giggles and exclamations of gleeful disapproval.

"Something wrong? Dear, you're positively blushing. What is it?" Bonnie arched a perfect eyebrow, lips curving as she shifted her gaze to Sarah. "Why, what a lovely necklace you're wearing tonight. A gift from Ron?"

Sarah nodded, her cold fingers grasping the glittering ruby as she reached for water with her other hand. After taking a sip she nodded again. "Yes. He's been working so hard lately, long hours. He surprised me with a present the other day."

"Well, it's really exquisite. So thoughtful. Though I suppose it's really a bit of a guilt present, wouldn't you say?"

Sarah clutched the gem and forced herself to look at her friend.

Bonnie's teeth gleamed between red curving lips. "I mean, he's ignored you for so long. Because of his work. Of course."

Sarah froze, betraying tears forming, the trapped fly waiting for that final agonizing moment. *I'm suffocating,* she thought.

"Oh, for the love of God." Bonnie raised her hand and snapped her fingers impatiently.

The young waiter appeared, attentive at the thought of an improved tip.

"Get the manager. We can't have that homeless fellow dancing here. It's positively disgraceful." Bonnie barked commands and then waved her napkin under her nose. "I can smell him from here. Disgusting."

Sarah noticed the unshaven, thin man standing near the wrought iron entrance to outdoor seating. His face glowed with the rapture of sound, every piece of him existing for the moment, the rest of the world abandoned.

~

The woman's shrill voice penetrated Bradley's dance. He didn't like looking at people's faces. Eyes sometimes burned. Words cut holes into his soul, down deep where the darkest part of him lived. He was afraid that the dark part might get loose and he'd have to see it again. Then he would have to stop being Bradley and become that other man.

But he looked anyway. Seamless faces, all the same, like judgmental dolls. All but one. He saw deep pools, a silver droplet flooding one. He traced the gentle stream down the end of a lash, over a delicate cheek where it defined a carefully hidden line in her soft flesh.

He recognized the silent scream. He'd seen it in a dark broken window, reflecting shapes and sorrow. Bradley moved his tongue, loosening the space around his teeth and gums. He snaked it out, just enough to moisten his lips. Then he moved.

~

"I can't believe it," Bonnie gasped. The others slid their chairs backward as though avoiding a careening train.

Sarah remained transfixed. The man moved closer, black eyes filled with unrecognizable tenderness. He held out a hand, grey and thin. The blood pounded in Sarah's ears, drowning out the world around her.

"Dance." It wasn't a question. As the word penetrated, Sarah felt something inside shift. One movement could set her free.

The glass slipped from her loosened grasp, the spilled water washing the wine stain clean. The music swelled and hesitation fled.

Gary R. Johnson

"Legs on Market Square"

Jan Perkins

New Orleans

"Katrina was a warning from God, just like Sodom and Gomorrah!"
The laments died down and the debris was cleared for rebirth of a
seductress that has captured countless hearts.

I will forever cherish pre-hurricane memories when the French
Quarter teemed with tourists as bright summer days began and the
heart of the Crescent City pounded with enchantment and intrigue.
Clowns performed on the streets. Bands played outdoors. Artists
painted in Jackson Square. Tap dancers drew audiences. The mingled
aromas of chicory coffee and fresh French bread drifted from cafes.

From mid-morning to mid-afternoon the stench from stacks of
bagged garbage along streets too narrow for receptacles fouled the air.
Sweltering heat and smothering humidity created a fetid, suffocating
sauna.

By mid-afternoon trucks cleared the littered curbs. Clubs opened
their doors and jazz flowed out. Beautiful sounds, soulful and strong,
echoed the agonized travail of their birth; music has carried the
haunting cries of the suffering oppressed down through the ages.
Maspero's Sandwich Shop was built around the original slave auction
block.

Drag queens and their papas roamed the streets, arms entwined. A
big bull-dyke bouncer barked from the doorway of one of the strip
clubs for passersby to come in and see the nearly nude female-looking
dancer on the bar. She touted her as "the biggest titty in the city."

Then sundown stole all innocence and the Big Easy turned sleazy.
Pushers and addicts found one other. Shrewd black pimps managed
from street corners their little white honeys, lost children coaxed to be
wasted women. A sign in a Decatur Street hotel window said, "All
street girls bringing in tricks must pay for rooms in advance." Sex was
ruthless business there.

The more privileged hookers worked from Lucky Pierre's Piano Bar.
They were all female with makeup-masked vacuous faces. They were

otherwise dissimilar, some looking like high school cheerleaders and others like Sunday School teachers.

Some clubs' walls were plastered with male prostitutes who looked like beautiful women. There rednecks got picked up and then went home with ribald tales of how they had been hoodwinked. Those who heard the tales could never be certain who the real impostors were.

At sunrise sinners went to mass at St. Louis Cathedral, confessed their sins, and resolved to sin no more. I imagined them finding their way home to their own beds to sleep in righteous peace in the city that care was supposed to forget, the city some say is a whore that got her just fate but others know as a saint in powder and paint.

Shannon Jones

"Natasha and Shannon: Silly Faces"

Christine Parkhurst

Book Club

A group of women — nine teachers, two engineers, one writer — a gathering as intense as any coven, meet every full moon around a long oval table to eat, drink, discuss books and the world, enjoyably, in any order or all at once.

Tonight we share Chinese food (wonderful dumplings!) and chilled white wine
   and dissect Amy Chua's new book,
      Battle Hymn of the Tiger Mother,
       about how Asians raise their children strictly, to win,
   compared to the Westerners' more laissez-faire attitude toward the game of life;
      the book's view is as black and white as the typed pages, with little room for gray
      although a Jewish husband's thrown in here and there for a splash
of color.

Though we are all Caucasian, no one was born in Tennessee
   and our backgrounds vary as much as our hair color
      (one platinum, two Titian, eight brunettes,
      and the hostess a natural redhead, just so you know).

Ah, Oak Ridge, with your core intellectual elite,
your nuclear physicists, math professors, oncologists!
    We wives in our fancy brick houses
   built ever-so-slyly atop hills of fire ants,
   look egotistically out at the world of words:
some jab wooden chopsticks now, fierce,
   angry to be so harshly judged
when the children, don't you know, came out just fine,

with not a battle scar to be seen;
others, like myself (having fought the Suzuki battle repeated times
with my own daughter and in the end, yes, sadly, having lost),
pinching more gently at the pot sticker,
    appreciating perhaps slightly more where Ms. Chua came from.

I'm a native San Franciscan,
        raised near that city's Chinatown,
        familiar with its early morning sour smells, the watered-down
cracked sidewalks,
            the open-fronted stalls stuffed with myriad imports—vivid reds
and blues,
                all crowded, noisy;
        chickens hanging headless by their feet in long straight rows
        over tins of curly black dried snake gut;
oranges round as breasts stacked in perfect pyramids;
and stray dogs sniffing for gingered garbage along narrow alleys
(I often prayed for their safety).

We empty the Chablis,
open our fortune cookies "in bed" and laugh and talk,
now frivolous, now serious,
ivory candles burning slowly within their bell jars,
flickering in the darkened room
(*I forgot to turn the light on in the china cabinet,* remarks our hostess).

    We, hovering over the book,
know we live in the heart of a once-secret city
still not daring to say a word
about the real world,
        the new truth of globalism built upon the razor's edge of chaos,
            1984 revisited.

So far from our varied novel reviews,
our diverse backgrounds,
our (gray) child-rearing practices
   is Mother China:
like a silent yet omnipresent neighbor covertly squatting on our
land, fire ants or not,
   she weighs in deep, preying on my mind as we read aloud and joke.

   With quick short puffs our hostess blows out the candles
at ten o'clock. I drive home, alone under a red-ringed moon,
the air clear and clean from recent rain,
my mind a jumble of remembered cacophony.

Judy Lee Green

Rice and Breath

Mute as a mannequin in six inches of snow,
he wears unfamiliar clothes: neon green
fleece-lined Snoopy jacket, Barney
cap with purple earmuffs, red cowboy boots.
His new brothers make snow angels, sled,
slide, run, play, shout at him to join them.
He doesn't hear, but huffs tiny breaths
again and again, fascinated, fearful that
he will run out of little smoky puffs. From
Haiti, he has never felt cold, seen snow.

He remembers when the earth shook.
In line to get rice, he and his *maman*

were struck by rubble. Her last breath,
a loud groan, tickled his ear but he did not
laugh. He shook like a scared donkey. Now
he has as many breaths as grains of rice,
a new home over the clouds, a new mama
and daddy, brothers. And little smoky
puffs of air that never run out. America, truly
a land of plenty, a land of many breaths.

Christine Dano Johnson

Houri

Late one fall, Aref began insisting that we run every morning, right after we dropped the children off at school. He had recently begun working second shift, and didn't go in to the hospital until 1:30 or 2:00 in the afternoon, before Atash and Noor got off the school bus.

I felt he was evaluating our little routine, similar to the way he assessed the residents who reported to him at the hospital. I always envisioned them with imaginary tails between their legs as he spoke to them. His voice could be sharp.

Usually, I began each day by waking the children, speaking softly and turning on their lamps. They knew this was their cue to rub their eyes, head downstairs, and begin the attempt to eat the bowls of Cheerios and rice milk that were waiting for them at the kitchen table. While they were eating (or rather, holding their spoons in mid-air while still dreaming), I would make their beds and lay out their school uniforms.

It had always gone smoothly enough; they kept their whining to a minimum, though we didn't try to be hushed and quiet. Aref was already in the hospital parking garage by that time, steering his silver BMW sedan into his assigned parking space.

That first morning home, arms crossed, an amused smile dancing on his effeminate lips, he observed me. His hair, still coal black, stuck up a little in the back and a white feather from his pillow was peeking out from the crown of his head. He hadn't slept off his Sunday-self yet; the hard edge that grew over him like kudzu during the workweek was not yet near.

I was dressed already. Not dressed up, just a pair of jeans and a long grey cardigan over a t-shirt. I didn't have a headscarf on or my manteau on over my clothes yet.

"Houri. Why don't you have the children make their own beds? They're old enough; Noor is in the third grade already."

I smoothed out Atash's little blue polo shirt, pausing and running my hand slowly over the little crest patch. He had just started kindergarten, and his wide brown eyes pleaded with me every morning to let him stay home. Home meant cookies and cartoons. School meant lots of noisy children and lines and loud bells. In spite of his fear, he seemed to like his teacher; she was young and soft-spoken.

"It's just faster this way, Aref. They get a little bit of food in them before I drop them off. Gives me a chance to make sure they have everything they need."

Aref shook his head a little and started pacing. A speech was coming. I wanted to get down to the children, to talk with them a bit before I had to start nudging them to brush their teeth and get dressed and zip their backpacks. I needed coffee.

"They should start making the beds by themselves, and also I want you and me to start running on the greenbelt after they're dropped off. It isn't so hot this early, and we both can stand to lose a little bit of weight."

He looked at my hips then, which admittedly had grown fuller and rounder over summer. The children and I had eaten lots of lunches downtown while Aref worked during the day. I always ordered dessert.

Already I felt the road that his mornings off were sending me down. My quiet, yellow sunlight moments were disappearing, and were being replaced by Aref's heavily structured, well-balanced efficiency plans.

No more novel-reading in an hour-long bubble bath. I would now have company as I cleaned, while I sat at the computer, and as I stepped outside to check the mail. I sighed and bit my lower lip as Aref outlined his plans for our four hours together before I left to pick up Noor and Atash and he left for his shift.

"Oh, Houri, don't frown so much . . . it will be nice! Haven't you been lonely in the house alone?"

"No. I am not lonely."

Aref's smooth face fell, and his lower lip pushed into a pout, a look that our daughter Noor had perfected at the age of two.

"We'll start running. It will be fun to have some time alone, like before the children were born."

Aref looked at me, his eyes crinkling up at the corners. I was still amazed at the length and thickness and the inky black of his eyelashes. I turned away from him and pulled a pair of Atash's small white socks from his dresser drawer. I could hear Noor laughing gleefully from the kitchen table, then a rustling, which was followed by an annoyed *"Hey!"* from Atash. I needed to get downstairs. We were behind schedule now.

"All right, Aref. We'll start running."

Charlotte Pence

The Myth of Balance

A sunny June morning,
all quiet streets and bird calls.
I sit on my front porch,
ubiquitous fern above
musters a quarter-turn—

stops—ponders—and then changes
its direction. Last night,
my neighbor stood on her deck
and cried so silently
hers must be a practiced art.
She stays with her husband,
believing in change, and that
good exists in each marriage.
Nothing will change, I would like
to say, except the weight,
increasing, from all the years,
like anvils chained to feet,
making you believe that house
is the one place for you.

Her son, Timmy, slams outside
and plucks his bike from where
it has lain in the front yard.
Now, no helmet, back flat,
head up, he races away
only to return soon.
I sip my coffee and read
another news story
of yet another war, more
rumors of genocide,
and tell myself this too will
be mitigated somehow,
believing in Balance—
that thin circus man on stilts—
to step in as needed,
center the flying see-saw,
stop any real disaster or change.

But haven't I been shown
Balance does little? The myth
leaves me alone to read,
wait for the neighbor boy
who now must be speeding down
that hill on 16th Street.
I saw him a week ago,
unable to slow down
at the intersection
at the hill's end. Hard tilt
of his body to the right,
so close his kneecap shaded
the asphalt, so close I
must believe in something,
or else why didn't I call
after him this morning?
Brake going down that hill;
stop hurling yourself down
trusting all works out in the end.

Judith L. Duvall

Different Rules

One August afternoon in 1946, the heat from the sidewalk burned
through my sandals as I walked the long blocks to my piano lesson.
My satchel, loaded with practice books, sheet music and a one-dollar-
fifty-cent lesson fee, thumped against my bare leg. Sweat covered my
skinny, nine-year-old body. Each week I dragged myself the ten blocks
from our home in Highland Park to Oak Street, where I played scales
and learned simplified classical music pieces from Miss Ruth Graves. I

didn't look forward to these lessons, and today I was especially miffed at having to give up an afternoon splashing through backyard lawn sprinklers with my friends. As I neared the corner of Oak Street, someone called out to me.

"Where you goin'?" came a soft voice within the deep shade of the corner house lawn. A girl about my age sat in a red Radio Flyer wagon under a large tree.

"Where you goin'?" she asked again.

I stopped and stared at her. She seemed like a nice girl, and of course I knew where I was going, but seeing her in that Radio Flyer left me speechless.

"Uh, I'm going to my piano lessons," I finally stammered, eyes fixed on the shiny wagon.

"'Guess you goin' Miz Graves' house, huh?" She looked at me, one hand on the wagon handle, the other holding a bottle of Grapette.

"Yeah, she's my teacher. Do you know her?" I asked, not taking my eyes from the wonderful, shiny red wagon.

"Yeah, she know my mama; gives me books to read sometimes," she answered. The girl took a sip of Grapette and asked, "What's you name?"

I told her my name and asked hers. "Sally Jane, but my brothers call me Sal," she answered, and drank more of the soda.

We sat in her wagon and talked. We learned we would both be in fourth grade, and she had three older brothers and a sister; I had one sister, three years old. We both liked to read and borrowed library books from the bookmobile that came to our neighborhoods during the summer. We shared sips of her Grapette, and then we took turns pulling one another the last two blocks to Miss Graves's Victorian house.

When my lesson ended, Sally Jane had disappeared. As I passed the big shade tree, I looked for her, but only a rusty tin roof poked above the tall, thick bushes that surrounded her house and porch.

After that day, I hurried to my lessons, hoping to spend time with Sally Jane. A girl with her own Radio Flyer wagon was someone I wanted to be my friend.

~

When I had asked for a Radio Flyer wagon the past Christmas, I received dolls and prissy dresses instead. My parents said that wearing pretty dresses would help make a lady out of me, and a wagon would not. They claimed it suited boys better than girls. My piano lessons were also part of their plan to change my tomboy ways. I didn't think much of their plans, and continued to spend most of my time playing with the Spencer brothers, who lived two houses up the street from us. They had two Radio Flyers, two bicycles, and Red Ryder B-B guns. I planned to start with a wagon and work up to the B-B gun. I had new hope now that I had met Sally Jane, a girl my own age who had a Radio Flyer wagon. I was determined to find out how she got it.

My mother had drilled it into me that it was very bad manners to ask anyone where they got their clothes or toys, and for heaven's sake, never ask the cost of anything, ever! I would have to think of a plan that didn't involve asking the forbidden question.

After days of thinking about it, I had no answers. I came up with only one possible idea of how Sally Jane might have gotten her wagon. I wondered if Sally Jane had used magical powers. I heard a story at Sunday school about a man whose girlfriend cut off his hair, and he lost his man strength; he turned weak as a baby. I heard another story about a girl with long hair so magical that when she hung it out the window, her boyfriend climbed it like a ladder. The next time I saw Sally Jane, I looked closely at her hair. It formed short, tight curls in abundance, like mine, but hers were black and mine shone in a reddish brown color that my mother called auburn. Since our hair pretty much matched except for the color, I didn't see much chance of her hair being magical enough to get her a Radio Flyer. I would have to think of something else.

Thanksgiving came and went, and I became more and more desperate. It looked as if I would have to ask Sally Jane where she got her wagon so I would have time to plan before Christmas. I reasoned that since a Radio Flyer was not clothes and not exactly a toy, my mother's rule didn't count. I made up my mind to ask on the next piano lesson day.

When the day came, a cold rain fell. My mother bundled me up and forced galoshes on my feet. I'd quit fighting her about the galoshes when I realized I could walk in the street gutter and never get my feet wet. I splashed along to Sally Jane's, and as usual, she waited for me under the big cedar tree. She wore a brown coat and a brightly colored scarf tied around her head. No socks showed above the high tops of her scuffed brown shoes, and she smelled like the donut shop on nearby McCallie Avenue.

I plopped down beside her in the damp wagon and asked, "Sally Jane, how did you get your Radio Flyer? Was it a present last Christmas?"

"Sure was," she replied with a big grin. It didn't seem to bother her a bit that I asked. She was proud of that wagon, and like me, didn't really view it as a toy.

"Was it a present from your parents?" I questioned her further.

"Nah, ladies at the big church in town give it to me," she answered, then motioned for me to get out. She wanted me to pull her to the corner.

"What church in town?" I asked, grunting to get the wagon rolling.

"You know, that First Baptist Church on Market Street downtown."

"How come a church gave you a wagon?" I asked.

Sally Jane laughed, "You crazy, girl; no church gave me this wagon; some ladies that goes to that church gave it to me." She kept laughing at me, but I didn't pay her much attention. I tried to figure why church ladies gave away Radio Flyer wagons. This was important information, and I didn't have much time to get a plan in place before Christmas.

Sally Jane explained that the ladies brought the wagon to her house along with toys and some groceries. I remembered that my mother's Sunday school class packed baskets to give away at Christmas. However, those baskets were full of dried beans, sacks of flour, and cans of Campbell's tomato soup, and there were no toys in any of them. I wondered if our Baptist Church being in Highland Park and not downtown made the rules different. These differences presented a puzzle I was determined to solve.

Thanksgiving came and went, and I realized I needed to get answers or I would lose any chance I had of getting a Radio Flyer wagon for Christmas. That's when I decided this problem needed help from my only grownup friend, Angeline. She lived with us except on Saturdays and Sundays and was the boss of our house. My daddy used to be the boss, but after Angeline came, he would ask her things like, "Would it be possible to have dinner a bit early on Thursdays?" Before that, he just *told* my mother to have dinner early on Thursdays. One time when he asked her, Angeline told him she couldn't make a roast cook itself faster, and he'd have to eat a bowl of canned soup. I figured a big fight would result from that one, but Daddy just said that would be fine, and he'd look forward to a roast beef sandwich later. When he also agreed "not to make a mess in *her* kitchen," I knew things had really changed in our house.

Tuesdays, when she did the weekly ironing, were the best times to talk over my problems with Angeline. When the next Tuesday came, I rushed in from school, smelled soup beans cooking, heard "Stella Dallas" playing on the radio, and knew Angeline still stood at the ironing board. She ironed in the dining room so she could keep an eye on whatever was cooking in the kitchen. I sat near her, smelling the starchy steam vapors that rose from the hot iron as it glided over damp shirts and dresses. She liked to hear about my school day and what was going on with kids in our neighborhood. I could tell she really listened to me because she asked picky questions about my school lessons and why I called someone a name on the playground. Things like that.

Well, it didn't take long before I learned that Angeline was friends with Sally Jane's mother, and their last name was Fowler. Sally Jane Fowler. I had never even thought about her last name. Angeline said Sally Jane's daddy died and left her poor mother to raise five children "best she could." She said they probably even went to bed hungry sometimes. I couldn't get it into my head how someone with a Radio Flyer wagon wouldn't have supper every night, so I figured Angeline was wrong about that. Also, Sally Jane had extra food like Grapettes and donuts, which her mother let her eat right before dinnertime.

I continued with my story about Sally Jane's Radio Flyer and how the First Baptist ladies gave it to her and how I needed help getting the ladies at our church to give me one. Angeline began shaking her head and saying, "Lawd, Lawd." Angeline said some words different from how I did, but I knew that meant "Lord, Lord," and I would be punished if I said it except in a prayer or reading from the Bible. I liked it when Angeline broke rules, and I sometimes whispered "Lawd, Lawd" along with her when she repeated it over and over, as she did now.

She finished ironing a shirt and turned off the iron. She looked at me real hard as if trying to see inside my head. Angeline stared like that when she tried to decide about telling me something important. Studying my face helped her decide if I was ready to receive the information she was about to give me. She said she could tell by looking through my eyes into my mind and heart. I had tried to figured out how she did this but had been promised a spanking if I ever tried "the staring business" on my daddy again.

When she began twisting her apron sash, I knew this might be as good as when she told me Mrs. Johnson's big stomach had a baby inside who later came out named Martha Ann. I could hardly believe Martha Ann had fit inside her mother, but Angeline said all people fit just fine inside their mothers before they came out, which is what we call being born.

Angeline leaned on the ironing board, tapped her fingers, and stared out the window into Mama's rose garden. I started to worry that she had forgotten all about my problem, when she said "Lawd, Lawd" again and began telling me how people got different things in life for reasons known only to God Almighty. I waited for her to get around to the part of how I could get my wagon, but she kept talking about "them that has and them that don't" until, crushed, I realized she meant I was one of "them that don't have."

~

She was right. I didn't get a Radio Flyer wagon for Christmas. She advised me to "forget about it and not nag poor Daddy with any more wagon foolishness." It had always been a good idea to listen to Angeline, so I took her advice; I let go of my dream of having a Radio Flyer wagon. I pestered the Spencer boys for rides in their wagons and began thinking I might want a bicycle pretty soon.

When summer came, my parents took me to spend a few weeks at my grandparents' house. When we arrived at their place in Knoxville, my Uncle Ernest came out with my grandmother to greet us. He was a bachelor, which my daddy said is a lucky thing to be.

When my parents left, Uncle Ernest said, "Come along with me; I've got something I think you might like."

My grandmother smiled and watched from the porch as Uncle Ernest led me to the garage.

"Now, close your eyes and wait," he said.

I did as he asked and listened as the big door creaked and groaned open.

"Okay, you can look now."

I opened my eyes and stared. In the middle of the musty old garage sat a shiny red Radio Flyer.

"It was too big to wrap for Christmas," he explained, "so I saved it for now. It's probably best if you keep it here to enjoy when you visit. No need to say anything to your folks about it."

"Oh, boy, oh boy," was all I said as I stroked the wagon. My heart beat so fast I could barely breathe. "Thank you, thank you, thank you, Uncle Ernest," I finally stammered, "You are the best uncle in the whole wide world!"

We hugged real hard, and he said, "Every kid needs a wagon; now go try it out."

I pulled my dream wagon out of the garage and around the house. As I coasted my Radio Flyer down the sidewalk in front of my grandparents' house, I thought about Sally Jane and how happy she would be for me. I also thought Angeline would be glad to learn that I was no longer one of "them that don't have."

Debra Dylan

My First Baptist

During the long journey south
I feared
meeting farmers
and war losers;
instead I found
a seven-year-old girl
in a homemade dress
who was always singing about a man's bosom
and practiced dunking herself
in a full bathtub.
"You talk funny," she said,
as she pretended to smoke a candy cigarette.
She spat in her blue Mary Kay eye shadow powder
to make it creamy:
"I want to be just like Mom."

Melanie Harless

Sunday Conversation with My Neighbor

On Sunday, my neighbor comes over to say
the preacher preached against
voting for the liberals today
because we are a Christian nation.
She knows I am a liberal,
but still prays for my salvation.

I open a beer and offer her one
although I know it's against her religion.

We sit in pleasant silence for a while.
Then she proclaims the young preacher's wife
is dowdy and doesn't discipline her child.
My friend goes on to lament
that she is so tired of old Mrs. Trent,
who always sits beside her and complains
about her many aches and pains.

With growing excitement, she confides
there's a rumor that two people in the choir
are having a torrid love affair.
Also, she heard that young Billy McBride
has gotten a girl in trouble,
but everyone agrees that it's okay;
at least now they know that he's not gay.

My neighbor hopes this conversation
will spark my interest in going to church
and ensure my eternal salvation.
I say I find the Spirit for which I search
on my walks in the woods at the break of day,
but I thank her before she goes on her way
for caring about me anyway, even on Sunday.

Elizabeth Howard

Exotics

Essie, this is Ermadean.
You know that crazy couple across the road from me – Ledford and
Versie Bottoms?
Yesterday they come home with a jackass
in the back of the Ford pickup.
A right pretty jackass, I have to admit.
Doe-colored with a chocolate cross at its withers.
It'll fit right in with their zoo
if it can find standing room in the yard.
It'll never get a toehold on the porch,
what with all the Rhode Island reds, gamecocks,
and strange-looking fowl
I never saw the likes of anywhere else.
They doze and shed and shit,
crowing and clucking, biddies
of every stripe and color running here and there,
cheeping, getting lost from their mamas.

The porch is a pigsty.
A pig, that's something they don't have yet.
But they got goats—a white one, a fuzzy black one,
and one covered in leopard spots.
When it rains, the goats crowd
right up on the porch with the fowl.
You'll never believe it, but I've seen the black one
and the spotted one dancing on the hood of a rusty car.

Well, I gotta go now.
My guineas are potracking, kicking up a fuss.
I guess what it is—I forgot to feed them this morning.
It takes a heap of corn to feed all of them.
But they're the prettiest things—
pearl ones and white ones.
And I've ordered some keets with helmets.
Versie and Ledford say my guineas
make enough noise to wake the dead,
but it's nothing like the bedlam over there.
That pretty jackass brays just like all the others,
like the trumpet announcing the end of time.
Can you hear it? Well, step outside and listen.
Like I said, I gotta go.
I'll call you back after I feed my guineas.

Margo Miller

"Leader of the Pack"

Laura Long

Brutal

Folks warned that winter was going to be brutal.

Syrah stood at the gate and waited, thin lower lip trembling, two long pigtails twisted into weird angles down her back. It was August and nearly sundown, still ridiculously hot. Clouds of red dust, kicked up from the crowd, floated by. Two women in faded denim jumpers called out as they walked up.

A tobacco-stained hand clapped down on Syrah's shoulder. "You ain't old enough to be married and your Momma didn't sign your paper," one of the women in denim said. "Who gets the money?"

"Uncle," she answered, scratching the back of her head, hoping the itch did not mean she had lice in her hair again. "That okay?"

The women looked at each other, then out at the crowd. Two bearded men grinned at the gate, both of them nearly toothless, waving fists full of green. The gate had loops of barbed wire on the top, new and probably stolen from a construction site. Part of the gate was shaded by overgrown sumac shrubs. Dark blistered berries swung on the branches.

Escorted, Syrah entered the fenced enclosure and handed one of the women a piece of crumpled paper. She shifted her weight over to her right foot and wiped her nose on the sleeve of her damp cotton shirt. She was hungry as a bear, but that was common in the mountains and maybe more so in Cocke County, Tennessee. Jobs were scarce; desperate folks had bad ideas and fighting cocks aplenty for making a little cash. Churches knew how to throw down a few snakes and pass the collection plate.

Some folks became experts at talking to kind people at red lights. Some girls, even the not-so-pretty ones, knew how to catch a man's eye and imagination when he was pumping gas into his truck at the gas station. Lately, even though the summer sun was still high in the sky, it

seemed leanness itself walked the hills, looking for a few dried
blackberries or hoping to steal some tomatoes or onions to make soup.

Appalachian winters, though, were always relentless. In December,
gray skies clutched the mountains, and in January, snow followed hard
with waves of white fear. By February, the worst month of all,
everything became blue ice: roads, rocks, trees, streams.

Although born and raised in Black Holler, Uncle didn't know how to
make moonshine, so his job in colder months was finding cock fights or
dog fights to bet on. The money he made on a few well-chosen wagers
could buy cornmeal, lard, apples, coffee, and cigarettes to last until
March.

Syrah narrowed her eyes. The enclosure was no more than 20 feet
wide with a flat, sturdy industrial fence. There was no grass, just dusty
clay dirt.

Uncle gripped the outer fence with his left hand. The fingers of his
right hand were gone, and the shriveled stump hung by his side. "Fists
up, Boo!" he called. "And don't turn your backside on it."

Syrah pretended not to hear. Last-minute advice wasn't going to do
any good. The only thing that mattered now was a high tolerance for
pain. What Uncle had said to her months ago was far more valuable:

"*If it is a goat?*" he quizzed. "*Could be anything, you know.*"

"*I will dodge it. It will ram itself bloody on the fence.*"

"*If it is a mule?*"

"*I will grab his mane and climb on his back and dig my thumbs into his
eyes.*"

"*A snake?*"

"*I will strike first, Uncle, behind the head.*"

"*A large spider?*"

She laughed: "*It won't be a spider. That would be no contest if I have shoes
on.*"

"*Damnation, child!*" Uncle shouted. "*Some spiders in Black Holler are big
as a pie plate and can jump like frogs! They will fly in your face and climb
down your throat!*"

The green shed was in the back of the enclosure, partially hidden by more overgrown vegetation. Honeysuckle vines and stunted mimosa trees gripped the sides of the shed as if trying to lift up the box and shake out the contents. Syrah was led up to the center of the enclosure, to an "X" mark on the ground. A strong breeze blew through, thick with the promise of rain, and the door on the shed trembled. Carpenter bees flew out of the roof of the shed and into the door, angry at being disturbed. The fat black bee-bullets bounced off and zipped into the woods beyond the fence.

Syrah looked down at her hands, rough, red, and calloused. A fly crawled along her moist forehead and eyebrows but she did not blink. She hoped there was not a wolf in the shed. She had seen pictures in books. Wolves were cunning and vicious; they chased animals three times their size, nipping at them and taking little bite after little bite until their victims' intestines hung down to the ground as they strained to run.

~

The denim women stayed close to the gate. The shed was still now, as if holding its breath.

"Let's begin," a denim woman said. She clicked a timepiece. "Ready?"

Syrah spat on the ground and did a little two-step jog forward and back. Men and women outside the fence shouted and clapped and began giving extra money to a man in a gray coat by the gate. A flock of noisy starlings began to gather in the closest trees. The denim women spoke a little louder. "We will exit the gate. You must open the shed door. Your body is the only weapon you may have."

Syrah nodded and the women wasted no time getting out. The gate swung shut and Syrah was already at the shed door, gingerly turning the rusty knob. Squirrels chattered from the trees and she heard the sound grow and grow in her head until it became her own heartbeat in her ears. The red clay dust breathed, sent clouds swirling in and out of the fence as more people gathered.

Syrah kicked the door hard and it swung open, slammed against the wall of the shed.

She peeked in. Nothing was standing there. Nothing clinging to the wall, either.

"What? Where's it at?" She searched faces in the crowd. "Where's it at?"

The denim-jumper women were at the gate, pushing people back. Syrah continued to search the crowd at the fence for a familiar face. "Uncle? Uncle!"

By then, the first fire ants were on her legs, stinging all at once. The burn was like poison ivy or poison oak, when it strikes in the middle of the night with itch and agony. Syrah fell on her knees and the ants met her there like a red carpet. Her rough hands were swift to grind many of them into a red smear, but there were so many, so many, pouring out from under the shed. As ants died, the pheromone alarm went out from their crushed bodies, exciting others to sting, calling more ants to come out from the ground.

A churning red mound formed and Syrah attacked it with her hands. Angry ants swarmed in the heat as their tunnels were torn open and laid bare by her fingernails. Wrinkled ant babies scattered like sparkling white seeds in the fading sun. More insects spilled out and flowed up from under the crusty clay. Syrah's legs were swelling from the first attack, her knees dark and plumping up like ripening fruit. She was sick and dizzy from the heat and dust. Her chest felt as if someone heavy were lying on top of her.

Crawling with movement, her arms turned prickly and she frantically scratched the welts. The fire ants held tight with their pincers and turned around in circles, stinging with throbbing abdomens, injecting venom again and again. Thousands of new ants arrived, and stingers filled with fresh poison met her pale, freckled skin with precision. Each sting sent a message to all the other ants to sting more, sting faster, turn in a circle faster, make more welts. Syrah clutched her chest, straining to fill her lungs with a full breath. Ants clustered under her arms and the pain went from her back to her buttocks in one lightning flash. She fell again, turned her head to one side, threw up.

Groans of disgust and disappointment went up from the crowd. Men cursed and began to leave the enclosure. Women wailed, mostly for the money lost. A one-eyed boy pointed a finger and giggled.

Uncle drew a moonshine flask from his coat pocket, took a long drink. So much depended on this. Winter was coming.

The ants reached the girl's mouth before the screams escaped.

Shannon Jones
"Untitled"

Barbara Bloy

Mommy's Doll

Mommy never did tell us much about when she was a little girl, but it was easy for me to picture her because she still has pigtails like us—she makes six braids every morning—except she doesn't let hers hang down or tie ribbons on the ends. She always pins them on top of her head like a crown.

We also knew that she had a twin brother, Uncle Russell, the freckled, friendly guy we sometimes saw at Gramma's house, and lots of boys on her block to play with, maybe because her father was a gymnast who fixed up a gym in the basement of their row house and taught them all how to do things on rings and mats and parallel bars.

Our only boy neighbor is Bobby Lee, and he's too big and serious, and then there's my little brother David, but he's pretty little, so he doesn't count. I have a big sister, too, Kathy—but all she likes to do is swing on the swings and play dolls with her friend. I'd rather go roller skating on the sidewalks, especially the ones made of slate that make such a fine hollow sound under my wheels and jangle my whole self when I fly over a crack. I *do* like to swing, especially singing songs that match the beat of the swishing air that pushes me from behind on the way up and blows in my face on my way down, but I don't see the point in playing house with cribs for the dolls and a tiny stove and a tea set on a tiny table. My favorite doll is a stuffed cat who doesn't have any clothes to fool with the way baby dolls have.

Seems like Mommy was more like me. Except she had a beautiful doll that had been our Gramma's when *she* was a little girl, and she kept it on top of the chest of drawers in her bedroom in a place of honor. She was a big doll with a head made of china and a soft body. That china head made her look almost real. Kathy's dolls all have rubber or cloth heads and their skin is either too orange or too white, and besides, they all have big red circles on their cheeks and they all cry "Mama, Mama, Mama" all the time. But Mommy's doll had blue eyes with real lashes and a perfect tiny nose and a mouth that looked like a regular mouth instead of being too red, and her cheeks looked like everyone else's. And she didn't cry—she didn't say a word. She wore a long white dress like she was going to be baptized, all dressed up and older than a little baby. She had real little panties under the dress that buttoned in the back with one tiny tiny button. But she didn't have shoes, and some of Kathy's dolls have them and even socks. I remember that every December Mommy took the doll from her dresser at Christmas time, and then she just sat there high up on the mantle in the living room. We weren't allowed to touch her even.

Well, Kathy, she's bigger than me, had her birthday in March, and all of us had lots of the cake with eight candles and ice cream on the back porch. Kathy got lots of presents and David and I got some too. After all the presents were opened, Mommy went inside and brought out a big mystery box. She helped Kathy open it, and inside was her doll. Mommy said that Kathy was getting old enough to know how to care for her things, and that she was careful with her nice tea set and she always tucked her dolls into their cribs at naptime and bedtime. And so she could have the doll with the china head for her very own. She told us that the doll was very old—it had been Gramma's before it was Mommy's, after all—and very easy to break.

Well, what *happened* is what I'm trying to get told. Kathy seemed afraid to touch that beautiful china face. While Mommy was telling us how much she and Gramma loved the doll, Kathy kept fooling with the paper it was packed in. But then Mrs. Price came out on her porch and Kathy grabbed up the doll all of a sudden and ran down the porch steps, out the gate, and down the driveway to show our neighbor. She was running and cradling the doll and calling to our good-as-a-real grandmother.

But then she fell, right on her face in the gravel drive with the doll still clutched in her arms. And she cried, screamed. Later I saw her hands and elbows and knees—boy, did she get scraped up. My brother and I huddled together, and Mrs. Price just sort of stood on her porch and played with her apron. But Mommy *ran*. And picked up Kathy and hugged her and brushed the gravel from her hurts and hugged her again and — I'm sure of this — Mommy was crying, too. We saw her face as she carried Kathy into the house, though she was trying to hide it, and we didn't want to look at her anyway.

When we looked back at the driveway, there was the doll — her china head smashed. Mrs. Price smoothed down her apron and went and picked up all the pieces, very carefully, even though there were so many pieces there wasn't any reason to be careful: nobody could ever get it glued back together even if you wouldn't have minded all the cracks, which I sure would have. She was a *beautiful* doll. Maybe that's why mommy cried.

But why didn't she even look at her when she ran out there? Why didn't she pick up the doll instead of Kathy?

Jennifer Hollie Bowles

"Sisters"

Dick Penner

"Santorini, Greece"

Jo Ann Pantanizopoulos

Vrehi sta Vrastama

It's raining in Vrástama

Vréhi sta Vrástama. It's raining in Vrástama,
cloaking that little village in heavy gray clouds.
The rainwater must be traveling fast down

their steep cobbled streets, rivulets in abundance
watering millions of olive trees on their way to the sea.
I see lights flickering through the night.

I wonder where the old man lives,
the one who finds us sitting under the sycamore
sipping our tiny cups of strong coffee, trying
to catch a cool breeze in the shady café. He knows
we are from somewhere else, strangers, *xenoi*.

We tell him we are from *Ameriki*, but we could
have said another universe, and it would be the same
to him, who never left *Vrástama*, never left his
grown daughter, paralyzed, forever bedridden,
forever a puzzle. *Why me? Why me?* he asks.

We squirm with no answer and offer him a seat,
knowing his tale of anguish will choke our moment of calm,
ruin our sweet coffee respite from the heat. We nod to
offer him hopes for a cure, trying not to absorb his despair.
Dark clouds move over the mountain, and big drops fall
heavy through the sycamore leaves. We find the reason to leave,
thankful for the rain, the cool air, escape. *Perastiká* we tell him.

I hope he returned home to tell his daughter about the *xenoi* he met,
the Americans who send their love and wishes for a speedy recovery.

Vrástama is a small mountain village surrounded by millions of olive trees in
northern Greece.
perastiká = get well

Janet Browning
"Girl"

Patricia A. Hope

My Angel

I was seven the year I drowned.
It was my first time to go swimming.
I promised Momma I'd be careful.

The water was so blue, like Ms. Emma's
Silk dress she wore the night of our school play.

I remember I got there early before the pool opened.
Mary Jo did too. She was older than me, but we talked by the gate
While we waited for the lifeguard to let us in.

She came almost every day, she said, and I couldn't wait
To watch her jump off the diving board. She promised to teach me how.

Finally the gate opened to a hustle of sounds:
Screaming kids, the lifeguard's whistle, the splash
From a cannonball jump. Mary Jo jumped into the deep end.

She went under then popped up, rubbing her eyes and nose and she waved at
me.
It looked so easy. I walked closer to the edge.

A boy standing next to me jumped in and a big splash of water
Landed on my feet. I hesitated then jumped. The water enfolded me,
plunging
Me to the bottom of the pool. I could not come back up.

A giant liquid fist squeezing the breath from my lungs.
The pain, the panic would come later, nightmares of drowning.

Suddenly a hand reached for me,
Pulling me to the surface. I choked and gasped,
Coughed, finally seeing Mary Jo through my burning eyes.

I never saw her again.

Donn King

Royal Princess Hannah Rides Among Us

I watch my wife shopping at Wal-Mart. Janet slows as she passes a rack of frilly dresses appropriate for a small girl. She reaches out and lifts the delicate fabric, feels its texture, looks closely at it, but the expression on her face is not that of the typical shopper considering value and feel.

She looks at the fabric, but she focuses long past it, miles away to a small bedroom crammed with medical equipment, past the blue corrugated oxygen tubes, the compressors, the suction machine, the little heater that warms water for humidifying air, to the specially-made bed purchased by a children's charity to serve as the reclining throne for our princess, our daughter.

I remember when she was born. Hannah was so utterly normal, a real relief after the scare of the pregnancy. Hannah had been connected to her mother through a two-vessel umbilical cord instead of the normal three-vessel one, something that only occurs in one percent of all pregnancies. That discovery led to many tests to check for normally-developing kidneys, heart, brain, etc.

We didn't do an amniocentesis that could have definitively checked for abnormalities, because that carried with it some risk of inducing miscarriage. We had already had one of those, and the results of the test wouldn't have changed our decision to continue the pregnancy. I do not judge others who decide to terminate a pregnancy, but we already knew we could not bring ourselves to abort the child we already knew as Hannah, so why risk the test?

But we waited anxiously, always trying to divine her progress, her health, her development. All parents count the fingers and toes of their newborns, just as I had done before, but the count seemed so much more important this time, and I remember the sweet relief when the count came out matching the statistical norm.

Hannah epitomized life, and we captured some of it on now-outmoded videotape. We don't play the tapes much, because they make me cry, and because we fear tearing them up in the old VCR. But one of my favorites shows me sleepily lying in bed with three-month-old Hannah who has just joined me to awaken me. She is looking around, bright-eyed, mouth stretched into a typical baby smile, fascinated by everything, and she suddenly begins grunting, filling her diaper. I react by waving the suddenly fragrant air away, and Hannah looks pleased with herself, on the verge of laughing out loud. As she continues with her efforts I am the one who gives in to uncontrollable laughter.

She was the youngest of our five. The four older ones were born of previous marriages, so Hannah was the only one tied biologically to us both. I held her, fed her, played little baby games with her—all the normal things. We had even begun to feed her baby food in an effort to help her gain weight. I often slipped her small bites of ice cream, delighting in the way she smacked her lips and ran her tongue around to get every creamy drop.

Each time we went to the pediatrician, though, the doctor's brows knit just a little more, and she said, "Hmmm," a little more. Hannah wasn't growing fast enough, so at the doctor's request we brought her in once a week for a weight check. Her growth continued to lag, and she wasn't hitting the developmental benchmarks, so the pediatrician finally said, "I think we need to do genetic testing."

That's when we found that Hannah has a tiny bit of extra chromosomal material, something she has in common with only 15 to 20 other children in the world at any given time, at least as far as anyone knows.

I think of all this as I watch Janet slowly pick through the frilly dresses, trying to figure which one would fit Hannah if she could stand up, if she could walk, if she could dance the way most seven-year-olds do.

We can tell that Hannah understands things said around her. When Mr. Tom, her physical therapist, puts a large elastic band in her hand and asks her to pull on it, she does her best to hold on and pull with all her might. When he asks her to hold her head up as she bends over the foam bolster, her head bobs around like a maestro's baton as she strains the muscles in her little neck, trying to control it.

She understands, but she doesn't have the coordination to speak, or to gesture, to point, or even to swallow in a controlled manner. The feedings I treasured stopped when a swallow study showed she didn't close her epiglottis, and most of her food went straight into her lungs. She was eight months old, and she has not had a bite since; she is fed only through a tube that connects to a port in her abdomen like a USB cord feeding data into a computer. Now her food slowly downloads throughout the day, and she has ceased watching us as we eat, her lips no longer miming the movements that have become totally unfamiliar.

At therapy we see that she belongs to a hidden community, a world of children who are differently abled. These children have abilities; they simply differ from those of other children. In that small waiting room and those hallways, we relax a bit among people like us—people who do not look at our daughter and then quickly look away; who do not feel compelled to ask "what's wrong with her?" These people talk to her as if she is present in the room and smile at our daughter not out of pity but because they see how wonderful and perfect she is.

In this group, small talk revolves around challenges with nursing schedules, or sources for suction catheters, or the merits of various brands of split gauze, rather than preferred varieties of grass for the lawn, or good deals on gym memberships. We all know "Welcome to Holland" by Emily Perl Kingsley, and we all find comfort in it.

The children look at each other the way most children do, sizing each other up, asking questions out of innocent interest, spontaneously holding hands if they are able. They don't stare in amazement, as if at an exhibit at Ripley's Believe It Or Not. Hannah remains solemn, but the other children laugh and play in whatever way they can.

Hannah is right there in her wheelchair, next to another child in a wheelchair, and they eye each other. The other child smiles and waves a hand bent by muscular forces that refuse the commands of her brain, and Hannah's expression changes in that slight way I've come to recognize as a smile. The vagaries of her trisomy seem to have left the muscles that would normally create a smile relatively unresponsive, while leaving the ones that express surprise or frustration or discomfort working very well.

In this setting my wife doesn't get that far-away look in her eyes. Janet and the other mother discuss the intricate pattern Janet crochets for yet another lap throw for Hannah, and the two children turn their attention to SpongeBob making a rude sound on the television in the corner near the ceiling. I notice it's a bit high for those of us sitting in regular chairs, but just right for those citizens who dwell in the slightly tilted world of pediatric wheelchairs.

"Normal" has become a very strange word for us. When people outside the community contrast our child to theirs by using this term, it has the effect of a reverse N-word (as polite people reference it now), a prejudice of sweeping exclusion. I bristle at the implication there is something "wrong" with Hannah, although clearly she is not like other children. Just as a child with blue eyes is normal for a person with the blue-eyed gene, Hannah is normal for a person who has that extra bit of chromosomal material on the fourteenth pair. In fact, Hannah is extraordinary for someone like that, because most of the others with that extra bit are not alive or struggle with life-threatening issues she does not.

It may be cliché, but for us it is simply true: Normal is just a setting on a dryer, a town in Illinois. This is the new normal. I don't really know what normal is, since change is constant. I just know that this has become normal, including the complete lack of predictability, and we are just fine with it.

Human beings usually have 46 chromosomes arranged in 23 pairs, and those pairings form our blueprints. Scientists are still working out how much of individual characteristics result from genes (eye color, yes; preference for baseball over football, not sure), but it's certain that they determine much of what makes individuals unique.

When the complex process of meiosis kicks in after a sperm fertilizes an egg, sometimes one of those 23 pairs gets an extra chromosome, called a trisomy. When that extra chromosome occurs on, for instance, the thirteenth pair, it's called trisomy 13.

Trisomies happen frequently in human reproduction. Trisomy 16 is the most common, but it almost always leads to miscarriage. Down syndrome (trisomy 21) is the most common among those who survive to birth, followed by Edwards syndrome (trisomy 18) and Patau syndrome (trisomy 13).

Other factors complicate things. The trisomy may not be a complete extra copy (known as "partial"), and it may not occur in all cells of the body (known as "mosaicism"). The funny thing about mosaicism is that the mix can vary from organ to organ. Mosaicism dilutes the effects of the trisomy, and partial trisomy leaves out some of the effects altogether (although it can lead to some unexpected effects as well).

Hannah's chromosomes can be described this way: trisomy 14 mosaic partial. If she were simply labeled "trisomy 14," she would likely not be alive, since it is one of the more common causes for miscarriage. She completely dodged the heart defect that is usually part of trisomy 14, as well as most of the facial deformity. A blood sample showed about fifty percent affected cells, but there is no simple way to know the mix in, for instance, her nervous system.

Observation suggests her nervous system has a lot of affected cells, however. Her brain scan was so normal, doctors repeated it, but there seems to be an issue with her extended nervous system that prevents the signals from her brain from getting through. Coordination, you might say, is a bit of a problem.

"Normal," therefore, has meaning in statistical terms, and in that sense is useful. The subset of statistics that interests us, however, has little to do with the general population.

If "normal," our N-word, carries the flavor of reverse discrimination, the R-word ("retard") strikes us directly. When I hear the college students I work with, or even my generational peers, throw out the word "retard" to describe a person they deem to be subpar, that word has the same gut-punch impact for me that the N-word can have for aperson of color. Writing that, I feel as if I should wash my hands. The R-word repels me that much.

I don't know if Hannah understands everything she hears. She can't tell me, for one thing, and for another, I'm not sure how much any seven-year-old understands things people say around her. I know she hears and understands Mr. Tom's instructions, but I hope that she never hears and understands the implications of the R-word.

I hold, therefore, the paradox of wishing with all my being that I could give Hannah the gift of normal existence, while at the same time accepting her fully as she is. I don't regret anything, and I feel honored to have been given the incredible gift of caring for her. But at the same time, when I see children her age running and laughing and creating a challenge for their parents near us in Wal-Mart, oh, what would I give for Hannah to be able to cause me those kinds of challenges!

Janet glances at me standing in the aisle as those children stampede past, and for just a second I see the depth of her own pain and yearning for her daughter to be able to say, "I love you, Mommy." And then the moment passes, and we move on through the little-girl clothes, looking for the sensible V-neck T-shirts with no glitter appropriate for a 7-year-old who breathes through a tube in her neck. It's just the way it is, and that's okay.

Donn King
"Royal Princess Hannah"

Ray Zimmerman

Anesthesia

The surgeon's slender hands
repair my broken heart.
A woman in a long black dress
peers over his shoulder.

I've seen her before: awoke
on pavement at age twelve,
my bicycle in the ditch, the
front bumper of a car beside me.

The lady in black has come
for another dance with me.
Not yet, she says, *but I'll be back.*

Jane Sasser

Bone Sister

Who is she, this woman my age
with marrow like mine,
who fights renegade cells?
Part English, German, Cherokee,
did she grow up singing
in haylofts, running barefoot
through pastures, resenting
her spray of brilliant freckles?

Surely, like me, she's a mother,
a bearer and believer in life
who must wonder why blood
would betray its own stream.
In my dreams she wears
a scarlet scarf, waltzes alone
in a shaft of light, weighing
the untapped costs of my gift
of life. My bone sister.
When did she know that
she'd turned on herself?

Dick Penner

Dark Hawk

Plodding up Pleasant View hill toward infinity,
feeling gravity's challenge
I look skyward and see
a solitary dark hawk, feathered wingtips
like fingers spread,
riding the thermals, lofting, swirling into circles,
a gyre,
looping back, drifting,
gliding, floating aimlessly.
I trudge below, a lumbering tortoise.
"What is it seeking?" I ask.
For a moment,
I think it might be me.

Joan Parker MacReynolds

A Grandpa, a Boy and a Bird

The strange thing is that Grandpa helped me a lot just before he died when he couldn't talk much. He stopped talking completely after he moved in with my aunt and uncle, but he could say "okay" and "I love you" last spring when he lived with us: me, my mom and dad, and my smart-mouth sister.

They all nearly drove me crazy. Really schizoid. My sister is two-and-a-half years older than I am and thinks I'm stupid, and Grandpa had changed so much. I avoided them all as much as possible.

I figure it was the worst year of my life except for soccer, which I was pretty good at and enjoyed a lot. Most of the bad stuff happened before Grandpa died. After he died things brightened up a lot, but it wasn't because he died; it was because he taught me a lot about girls and things.

My biggest problems were that my sister mouthed off at me all the time about stuff that was not exactly her business; Grandpa moved in slow motion like his body motor was on idle; and everybody had a girlfriend but me. Then once in a while Grandpa wet his pants and if I was around, I'd have to be the one to take him and help him change. Those were the times he wouldn't look at me. That was okay with me.

The rest of the time he looked at me like my dog Baloney. Baloney can grab me by the eyes and not let me go when he wants something. Both of them have dark, damp eyes that can read your innards. Eyes like that in people can give you the willies. It's like being invaded by some weirdo shrink with no-name powers who can look around inside your head and blame you for whatever he sees in there: things you don't even know yourself, or things you, for sure, don't want to talk about. With old Baloney I can usually figure out what it is that he wants me to do. His brain pretty much runs between tennis balls and food dishes and wanting in or out. With Grandpa I couldn't figure anything out. But with Grandpa I did find out that if I just talked to him, it wasn't so bad. I could talk to him about anything. He'd say either "Okay" or "I love you."

The change happened when I invited Grandpa to eat breakfast with me. We have pizza almost every Friday night and Mom makes an extra pizza for breakfast Saturday mornings because I like cold pizza for breakfast. On that Saturday morning two birds had been singing so loud they woke me up and I decided to go out and see if I could find them. They sounded really big.

Grandpa was wandering around the kitchen when I got up, and I felt sorry for him and invited him to come outside and eat pizza with me.

"Okay," he said.

I helped him out the door and to his chair and stretched out on the grass to look for the birds. When I pointed them out to Grandpa, he looked up and dropped half his pizza on his lap. He stuffed the broken piece and a bite of loose sausage into his mouth, tried to pick up the tomato smear a couple of times and said "Okay" before his mouth was empty.

When I found them again and pointed, I think he saw them too. They were flashy redbirds—cardinals. The female kept flying away from the male, but he was never far behind. He chased her all around. I found her on a branch and watched him fly to her. Before she fluttered away again, he raised his crest and stretched his neck out like a would-be swan. Then he began to sway from side to side. She didn't fly this time. She swayed too. They looked like they were slow-dancing, and I turned to see if Grandpa saw them. He appeared focused.

The female was brown compared to the bright red male. Her red beak made her feathers look as drab as a dead leaf. I guess it's not how she looks that matters. They were singing back and forth whisper-soft and then like a CD turned up high in a car with all the windows down at a red light. He'd sing a song to her and she'd sing it back to him. Then he'd repeat it back to her and she'd add a note. It was a real show.

"Do you still see them, Grandpa? He's not giving up easy, is he?"

"I love you."

"I think he's trying to get her for a girlfriend. It's probably easier for a bird."

"I love you."

"Well, you're the only one. I don't have a girl. Every other guy on the soccer team has one except Dickie Palmer, and he stinks."

He shot me the Baloney eyes.

"I don't stink, but I get real red in the face if I even think about talking to this girl named Zoey. I can feel the heat in my head . . . it matches my hair. I hate it."

Grandpa didn't say anything.

"People call me 'Volt.' It started when I made a good soccer kick . . . . Well, I won the game for us and everybody looked at me. That was when Dickie Palmer yelled, 'Hey, look at Doug—he's got his high-voltage head on!'

"I started to yell, 'Yeah . . . . Well, Stench, you stink!'

"But things happened too fast. The team picked me up and the guys on the bench started screaming, 'Volt, Volt,' and then the cheerleaders and people in the stands picked it up and stomped their feet in time.

"I guess I'm a jock now, and I want to ask Zoey to come see me play. So far we only say things like 'Hi, how's it going?' But I'll turn as red as that crazy cardinal if I try to talk to her about coming to a game. My whole head will light up. I bet I even get red lips. Who could like a guy with a red head that goes off and on? The big question is, if I did ask her, would Zoey say yes to a red-faced, red-haired, red-lipped dork?"

"I love you." He was awake.

"You think there's any possibility she'd say yes?"

"I love you."

"I've been thinking I'd ask her to play tennis—she's on the tennis team—and I'd talk about soccer and see if she'd come to a game."

"I love you."

"What do you think she'd say if I asked her to play some Sunday?"

"Okay."

"You think?"

I almost missed his sentence. He didn't say sentences any more and I had to figure it out, and Grandpa spoke his words so slow that I had to concentrate:

"Okay. Work. Okay." He stopped talking.

Then he said, "Up. Okay."

Then he said two words together. "Some guts."

He paused a long time between words, but I put it together: *Work up some guts.* I kept looking at his face to see if he had any more words to say.

"Man," he added.

Then he just gave me that Baloney-eyed look and said, "I love you."

Work up some guts, Man. I didn't know what to say but it kicked me up into third gear. After that we ate our pizza breakfast together every Saturday morning until Uncle Frank picked him up. Just before they walked out the door, I went up to him and hugged him and whispered his words in his ear: "Work up some guts, Man."

His Baloney eyes locked on mine and he smiled a little. I smiled big. My parents and my smart-mouth sister couldn't believe he smiled. My sister wanted to know what I said to make him smile because he didn't smile any more either. Naturally, I wouldn't tell. It didn't shut her up, but I kinda liked having her run on. I felt in charge of something for once.

The next day at school I must have been wandering around in the hall about like Grandpa wandered in the house when Miss Pickett, the fast-walking librarian, slowed down beside me and said, "People are trying to steer around you to keep from running you over. If you don't want to be trampled dead in this hallway, you'd better watch where you're going."

I was still looking at the back of Miss Pickett's head when I heard someone say, "Oh, hi, Doug."

I automatically said "Hi" before I knew who spoke.

It was Zoey. My eyes went fuzzy and my brain crashed. My body felt like a volcano with red lava pouring out from the top of my head down over my face and ears and down my neck. I did at least make sense of some of her next words . . . something about me and tennis and a tournament. I managed to open my mouth and say a few words like "okay" and "yes" all stewed up together.

"Great, we'll talk," she said.

And when she turned to walk on down the hall, she turned her face back and smiled. I gave a smile my best shot. I didn't know what I'd said yes to, but if it had to do with Zoey, "yes" had to be the right answer.

Still, I stood rooted. The hall was clearing out and I needed to get on to class, but I couldn't move my legs or my concrete feet and I was still breathing funny. This situation reminded me of the cardinals. She sang and I wanted to answer and follow her, except I couldn't talk, walk or fly.

About the time I tested my right foot to see if it would move, Dickie Palmer stopped in front of me and said, "You all right?"

"Yeah, why?"

"You got your high-voltage head on . . . you know, like when something happens."

"Yeah . . . . Well, I'm okay."

"You better be, Volt. We got that big game tomorrow night."

As Dickie walked away, a mild aroma drifted along behind him. I thought, *If I'm Volt, you're Dickie Stench Palmer. Volt. Stench. Get it, Stench?*

In English class the next day, I walked in after Zoey and took a seat next to her. She usually spoke first, but this time I worked up some guts and made a move. I said "Hi" before she could speak. Then I asked her about the tennis tournament, and I think my head measured lower voltage.

She told me she wanted to practice with somebody besides Lissa because she knew all Lissa's plays. I heard every word she said this time and told her that I play soccer better than tennis, but that I'd be glad to help her out.

"Oh, great! Maybe I'll have a chance to win that tournament," she said.

We set the date and time and my father drove me to the court. I asked him please to let me out three blocks from the court and told him that I'd walk home.

"That's a pretty long hike," Dad said.

"It's okay. I can use the exercise."

"Your choice," he said.

I stopped practicing my serves when Zoey walked into the court, but I let her watch a couple before I stopped. At first I acted like I didn't see her coming.

"Hi," I said.

"Hi, yourself. You'll have to let me warm up."

"No problem." I didn't care how long it took her to warm up. I just liked looking at her and knowing that she was talking to me and nobody else.

"Why don't we not keep score?" I suggested. I had already figured that either way, I'd lose if we kept score.

She looked me in the eyes a second and then said, "Sounds good to me."

We played hard but she kept up with me and a few times played better than I did, but at least I made a couple of approach shots and some decent serves. I've played with guys better than me and learned a few things the hard way.

On the walk home I had plenty of time to think about my good luck and make plans for the future. I thought about Zoey coming to see me play soccer. I thought about that cardinal chasing his bird girlfriend . . . how it and Grandpa started me thinking. I thought about Grandpa and how he had spoken that sentence to me and how I'll never forget that thought. Ever. I remembered the slow motion and the long pause between each word. It was like a little kid trying to talk . . . like he said "Okay" to himself when he got each word right. "I love you, Grandpa," I whispered under my breath. *Work up some guts, Man.*

Not one of us had any idea that Grandpa would be dead the month after he left our house. It was an awful shock even though we knew he'd been sick a long time. I know things and people die, but I sort of don't believe it when it happens. It's like if I called him on the phone he'd still be there . . . but I know he wouldn't. Or that he'll come back to visit us in a few months . . . but I know he won't. Maybe it's because I can still see and hear him in my head that makes it hard to believe he's really gone.

Good news and bad news can get all mingled together. I've had to try to untangle my own mind. Grandpa drove me crazy for a while, but by the time Uncle Frank picked him up, we had a good thing going. He was my best older friend. It's funny how things can change like that.

He spoke his last sentence to me, and when I said it back to him, we were the only two who knew what we meant and where we stood. Together. I figure I miss him the most, and for some reason I don't think the Baloney-eyed look bothers me so much anymore.

As for my smart-mouth sister, I've found out that if I agree with her about my stupidity, it shuts her up like magic. It kills her that her stupid little brother made Grandpa smile and she doesn't know how. Besides which, I'm her stupid little brother who's an honor-roll soccer jock with a great girlfriend.

Penny L. Wallace
"Framed Images"

Eli Mitchell

From a Psychological Examiner
to an Appalachian First-Grader

Maybe Baby Jesus
did discover America

and maybe Christopher Columbus
is the High Sheriff.

Fur
does mean "way over yonder"

and you're right:
sometimes it rains frogs.

Marianne Worthington

Cousin Emmy and Her Kinfolks: Show Car

My brother-in-law always drove the show
car, knew how to navigate every pig
track and back road without a map, could drive
safe in cities, too. Drop us at the load-
out on time without a hitch. Cheerful he
was, and good-hearted, a big grin to match
his wit. But Lord, he had enough of South
Knoxville still in him to park that show car
at a tilt under Mam's old shed and prop
the door open, let his hunting dogs flop
in the back like a doghouse. So if you
were to come up on it, see that Cadillac
full of old yellow dogs, you'd think we were
right trashy. He kept the car shined up for us
and always tried to clean the seats, but we
were forever brushing dog hair
from each other's hind ends before a gig,
blonde swirls and hanks we picked like strings,
strummed off quick
as a drop thumb on the banjo.

Janet Browning

"Boys/Car"

Kesi Garcia

37876 – A Snapshot

Brown pickup, dusty school bus, red Camaro, shiny motorcycle, rusty
bicycle
Some back up, some pull in
Hoses fill tanks with gas
and tires with air

Door propped open by the cash register's line
Indian music dances through the air
Grease sizzles on the grill

The black suit buys the *Times*
The Copenhagen-scarred jeans take a stack of tickets
The matching sundresses lick vanilla ice cream cones
Gold chains totes a six-pack of Bud

The clerk reveals two gold teeth
and too much chest hair
to black suit: "Not want coffee with that, buddy?"
to Copenhagen: "No burger today, buddy?"
to the matching sundresses: "No candies today, babies?"
to the gold chains: "No tickets, *amigo?*"

Most say yes
but some say no
The line speeds up
and the line slows down
but the line never disappears

Judy Lee Green

The Dogtown Wishy-Washy

They came in Wranglers, work boots
and co-op caps, pull-on pants, kitten
sweatshirts and tennis shoes, carried Bibles
and musical instruments: guitars, fiddles,

mandolin, tambourine and doghouse bass.
Carpet factory work weary and burdened
by overdue rent, third time this year;
$2.99 for a gallon of regular; 24.9% interest

on MasterCard debt from last Christmas:
hoochie mama daughters, pothead sons,
they slumped on donated folding chairs
from the Fruit of the Vine Family

Outreach on the highway.
In the former concrete block
Dogtown Wishy-Washy, the music
began at the Holy Ghost Church

and the Spirit of the Lord came down.
Preacher played his high-school trumpet
from the Harbuck Marching Band,
stomped the devil with his feet, kicked him

out the door, passionately portrayed
for the small congregation of saints
the destination of a heavenly home
in the sweet by-and-by or the heat

of eternal fire and damnation.
Burdens lifted like grass stains
from weekend laundry, joy overflowed.
Lathered with hope, hips swayed, feet danced,

tired frowns turned upside down.
Limb-lean men and biscuit-bellied women
were filled with the Spirit, twirled and twisted.
Goodyear truck tires spun like Kenmore dryers
as the congregation departed, load lifted,
souls bleached spotless, pure and bright,
washed in the blood for another week
at the former Wishy-Washy,
Holy Ghost Church at Dogtown.

Patricia A. Hope

24 Hours with a Trucker

Today, I am the fly on the wall. The observer. The curious. The what-am-I-doing-here passenger in a 1995 Peterbilt with a 425-hp Cat diesel engine. I'm a reporter looking for a story but this assignment isn't like anything else I've done. For the next 24 hours I will be living on the road trying to figure out what it's really like to be a professional truck driver.

I'm in an all-American truck with an all-American trucker. A slightly overweight, average-height, 30-something white male with Southern roots. But he could be any size, any color, either gender. He's been from Montreal to Miami, from Hackensack to San Francisco. He has more miles under his belt than some astronauts. He even has his own language. He's street smart and road tough. Today we are taking a load of film to Atlanta and because film is perishable, we are pulling a "reefer," a 40-ton refrigerated boxcar on 18 wheels.

"I guess you could say truckers are a breed unto themselves," he begins. Shades hide the tiredness in his eyes but not the lines on his face from years of squinting into sunrises and sunsets, dealing with snow glare and fog, and downpours that obliterate everything beyond the hood of his truck. His cap is pushed back and covers most of the too-long hair curling out from the edges. He's wearing the red, white and blue symbol of his company, and his patriotism is displayed on stickers, cap and windshield. His sense of humor is evident in his laid-back drawl and quick and easy smile. The truck's console is a conglomerate of 13 gauges, 19 switches, 9 gears plus reverse, and 6 or 7 gauges just for the reefer, plus 7 mirrors, a CB, an AM/FM radio, and two heater units. The steering wheel is as large as a family-size pizza. His arms are huge. The hands are calloused. The ever-ready gloves lie on the seat beside him.

"We have a network, like a family," he says. "Usually you can count on someone to help you out if you're in a jam, but we're not as close-knit as 20 to 30 years ago. There's so much pressure today to get the load there. Meeting deadlines is very important. Like everyone else, we have too much to do and too little time to get it done."

I've been watching, listening as we head south on I-75 from his native hills of East Tennessee. His voice is soft but sincere as he flashes me a smile. "Just relax. We won't be into the bad stuff for a couple of hours," he laughs.

My eyebrows lift in doubt. The cars zoom past us at the speed of light, darting in front of us, braking with no regard for the tons of weight traveling behind them. "How do you get used to this?" I ask.

Before he answers, he switches on his turn signal and rolls the giant steering wheel to the left as we ease into the left lane to go around a mom-and-pop camper that's barely doing the minimum speed limit of 40. "I'm always looking for a way out," he replies. "It's my fault if I'm in a wreck. There are only two kinds of accidents: a few that aren't preventable and most that are. Professional drivers should be able to anticipate what may happen and know what they will do if it does."

He sees the "Weigh Station Ahead" sign and falls into line behind the other truckers, waiting to exit and satisfy the Department of Transportation that he is carrying only what the law allows. "Like anything else," he says, as he gathers his log book and necessary documentation, "there are a few bad apples but most drivers are good people. It's the people who prey on truckers that give us a bad name.

"Heck, there are drivers out here with college degrees—husband and wife teams that like the call of the open road, the excitement of not knowing what's around the next corner. It's no longer a redneck industry. There's big money being made out here."

"Is that why you do it?"

"Sure. I do it for the money but most of us couldn't settle down into an 8-to-5 job. It would be too boring. This way we get to have several professions." He pauses as a voice on the CB fills the cab. He adjusts the volume but doesn't turn it off. "We are part mathematician, part mechanic and part psychologist. But we've been called a lot worse!"

"And you like wearing all those hats?"

He nods. "The American truck driver avoids scales and delivers mail and wonders why we stay in this crazy business. It's not cheap. The cost of one fine can break you and no one feels the price of gas more than we do. It now takes nearly three-fourths of what we make."

"So, why don't you quit?"

He laughs. "Why don't you quit doing what you're doing? Don't tell me it's for the money. You're doing it because every story is different and you like the thrill of the chase. Am I right?"

"That, and I feel like I can make a difference for someone . . . maybe. At least I like to think so."

"Me, too," he responds. "Think about it. When you spend $100 for groceries, part of that cost is for the truckers who delivered your corn flakes from the snow-covered terrain of Michigan. The bananas you sliced into your cereal traveled from the tropics before some trucker picked them up at a Florida importer and sped them to the grocer's produce bin."

"I guess everything is affected by trucking," I answer.

"When you got up this morning, did you think about the fact that your TV, alarm clock and coffee pot were delivered by trucks? If you drove to work, did you consider that your car didn't get to your town or your favorite car dealer without a truck?

"Forgive the soapbox here, but if you expect to get the job done, be it placing flowers into an arrangement or pouring concrete for a bridge, some trucker delivered everything you depend on to get that job done."

He goes on. "Taking the family out to eat tonight? You'd have a hard time buying shrimp scampi in St. Louis if truckers didn't speed their reefers from the Southern fishing ports to the heartland. Despite the frustration, loneliness, anger, lack of sleep, and the aches and pains from sitting too long, some trucker took his job seriously and delivered the goods."

"I can see that," I tell him as I play the opposition, "but they still go too fast and kill too many people. They tear up the roads and jam up rush hour. Surely, more regulations are needed."

"There's a shortage of truck drivers now because of regulations," he responds. "State, federal, county, local regulations . . . all states are under federal, but then each state has its own. We can't do one thing in Georgia; in California it is something else. There's no ceiling on fines that are five to ten times more than they are for everyone else."

I wait for him to talk to the weigh-station official and provide the necessary paperwork. This time they pass us on through. We go around the truck in front of us. He wasn't so lucky. The dogs are sniffing his truck and several officials are talking to him. "Something wasn't right, I guess." He answers although I haven't asked.

"So, what would make it better? What would you change if you could?"

"We should be paid like everybody else—for the hours we work. Let us work 40 hours instead of 80 or 100, let us increase the size of our load and educate the public on the issues that truckers have.

"Take the time to know a trucker and you'll reject the innuendos that they are all out to run you off the road. They are single, married, missing their kids, loving their wives, longing for Mama's cooking and counting the hours left in their day just like anybody else. In fact, if all drivers were as professional as truckers, more people would get from Point A to Point B with their life and their sense of humor intact."

"Okay, I'm beginning to see that," I tell him just as some trucker swears an unrepeatable string of words over the CB. "You guys have your own lingo, huh?"

"Yeah, but most of it's just trash talk, a way of letting off a little steam when someone pulls in front of them or won't let them out into traffic."

"I hear the other truckers talking and I know that '10-4' means *okay* or *I acknowledge what you're saying*. I know that most cities have a nickname; that today we came through K-Town (Knoxville, TN) and Choo-Choo (Chattanooga, TN) and that we are headed to the Big A (Atlanta, GA), but even the lanes of the highway are named?"

"Sure. We're in the Hammer Lane now, which is the inside lane of a four-lane interstate. Ideally, the right lane, also known as the Granny

Lane, is for the slower rigs and four-wheelers. Now, as we get into Atlanta, you'll see that some of the far left lanes are restricted and truckers are not supposed to drive there. In some states they will barely let us out of the Granny Lane."

We pull through rush-hour Atlanta and the traffic resembles a phalanx of ants—tiny vehicles below us running at breakneck speeds to get to some unknown destination. The chatter on the CB is constant. The trucker uses the CB to find out what lanes are clear and what exits to take, and provides the same information to other truckers. We finally pull into the dock at the Kodak warehouse.

"What now?" I ask.

"We watch a little TV, read, sleep. You can have the bunk. I'll camp out here between the seats."

"With all this noise? I guess you don't get much sleep, do you?"

He chuckles. "You get used to it. Believe me."

He is right. I actually sleep better than in my own bed. But the banging down the side of the truck comes much too early. There is no pushing the alarm and rolling over. They are ready to unload us at 6 a.m.! The trucker pulls on his gloves and gets out to open his trailer for the dock workers. We then go inside the company's building to the trucker's lounge where fresh coffee, hot showers, television and morning papers await us.

"All the comforts of home." He chuckles at the relief on my face and the toothbrush clutched in my hand.

Later that morning, we deadhead out of Atlanta and the company sends us to a north Georgia town that eats, breathes and sleeps chickens. It would be great if we could go as the crow flies, but instead we traverse narrow roads through quiet little towns as we head for our destination. We pick up pallets, then go to the freezer company. We literally drive through the building, seeing chickens in every stage of life and death, to pick up our load.

"That's part of the excitement," he explains. "From film to chickens, I've hauled it all. I've had loads that didn't have a buyer; had one load go bad. I took it to the landfill."

But today it's chickens — 44,000 chickens, dead, frozen, packaged and palleted chickens that make us 80,000 pounds meandering the back roads of northern Georgia as we weave our way back to the interstate. We have a 1:00 p.m. appointment at a Georgia distribution center. We arrive at 12:55. We leave at 4:30. "Part of the frustration is the waiting," he says, blowing his horn for a little boy playing in his yard as we pass.

After dropping the trailer, we pick up another load and head north. I can't believe our 24 hours is almost over.

"I know a great little truck stop up the road that has the best steaks this side of Chicago. Ready for dinner?" he asks.

"Sounds good," I answer. We settle back, listening to the CB chatter. The sun is setting to our left and traffic has thinned out to a comfortable pace. The first weigh station we pass is closed.

"Doesn't make me mad," he chuckles, shifting the Peterbilt into high gear and pointing it toward home.

Pamela Schoenwaldt

Linguistics

My grandfather's grandmother was Chippewa. She wore hides. She ground Iowa corn. Dark, sticky blood of deer flowed over her hands. Black hair streamed loose behind her as she ran. I imagine this, for no name, photograph, or letters remain. I stalked my grandfather for stray words of her to braid them into a thicker tale and he said, "I already told you what I know."

I know that her people had rich, watered land, but they stayed too long, watching it fill with strangers. At first pale men came alone to hunt, drink, die, or wander west to the emptiness. The Germans were different. They came in flocks, waving papers, making signs, "See?" they said, "The land is ours now." They chased the deer away, cut high grass to black earth, ripped open the land and planted wheat. She watched from thickets as one man solemnly scratched rows in dirt. Sweat soaked through his woven shirt. She was perplexed by his toil when abundant food could be plucked from bushes, scooped from streams or whistled down from trees. Why trade grain for cloth if soft hides could easily wrap the body? Yet still she must have been uneasily drawn to his straight-arrow world and he to her wildness. They met at the fringes of his fields, found a way to speak together and began to fall in love.

"Why him?" her tribe demanded.

"Traitor!" said his people. "Have we come so far and worked so hard, tearing out grass to grow our food, that you must bring in dark disorder, hair unbound and a savage tongue to call down her brother-beasts on us?"

So he took her north to Canada where they both were strangers. He became a carpenter and worked in town. She learned German, copying his sounds as once in her warm summers she copied bird songs until only the owl discerned a human accent in the highest trill. Patiently, he molded her tongue with kisses, warmed her at night with new words, waiting until his ears discerned no difference in their speech.

Then he bought her dresses, ribbons, corset stays, light powder for her cheeks and pins to loop her hair in curls. They hoarded coins as her people hoarded corn in winter. At last he brought her down to another Iowa town where no one knew their story and all cautiously admired his elegant, black-haired woman. He built a house for her beyond the last roads, where the grass was still uncut.

But my grandfather's grandfather and this woman had been too long alone together. Their ears no longer caught the feather-edge of strangeness in her words.

"She's no German," the women whispered. "Listen to her. Look at her skin. She's one of *them*." Then my grandfather's grandmother feared that for this feather-edge she would lose her home again. But her lover did not flinch.

"She's Polish," he insisted.

In the way of small towns and because they needed carpenters, they left his lie alone and did not ask again. In time they made room for "the Polack" in her people's land. They helped her cook their stews and bread and adjusted her clothes and speech to be more like theirs. She, for her part, was careful to never make her people's food again, to speak her own language to her baby son or call down birds. Only at night, holding her, did my grandfather's grandfather hear laments he did not understand, cherishing her strangeness, familiar as no other.

Their son grew into a dark, hard man with a thin, hooked nose, for which sign he hated his mother and took care to import a pure German girl who soon betrayed him, learning the English he would not speak. So he became the foreigner, never tuning his heart to the wild strangeness, the new language of any love.

Melynda Moore Whetsel
"Tapestry II"

Judy Loest

Living *la Bonne Vie* in Tennessee

Did you ever set foot in a foreign country for the first time and know you were home? I had that feeling the first time I visited France. Riding the TGV through the French countryside, I was like Mark Twain during his own rail excursion there in *Innocents Abroad*—"Such gardens, such marvels of order and cleanliness!" "Such quaint red-tiled villages and mossy medieval cathedrals and turrets of feudal castles!" "To be in beautiful France . . . in all its enchanting delightfulness!" After all my exclamations came a kind of sweet exhalation—Ah, so this is where I was meant to be.

After my second trip, I developed a low-grade despair. I realized that I would never be able to live in France, that I would never have even a tiny *pied-à-terre* even in the fringes of the furthest *arrondissement, quel dommage,* not even on the same continent. What was I to do? For someone who feels a psychic connection to the French way of life, *la bonne vie,* someone who may, in fact, have been French in a past life, living in Tennessee is like . . . well, a real *malade au coeur.*

Despite exhausting Ancestry.com's ability to find my French ancestors, I am certain that somewhere along the torqued limbs of my Appalachian family tree there was a Frenchman in the woodpile. My brother, who is a Harley-riding, 180-degree opposite of anything remotely French, but who claims to have some experience with genealogy, advised me to enlist professionals. "Just send in the 25 bucks and have 'em run it back. They'll even throw in a coat of arms." "Run it back" has become a running joke in our family. "How can she eat that stuff?" we ask about an aunt whose favorite restaurant is Taco Bell. "Run it back," one of us will say. "Why do I think I deserve better than this?" my niece asks, bemoaning her life as a single mother with three kids and two jobs. "Just run it back," I say, and we hoot.

My mother, whose maiden name was Ramey (see? Ramey, a phonetic spelling of the French surname *Rémy, n'est-ce pas?*), has her own ideas about genealogy, based partly on the fact that her father was a moonshiner. Whenever I mentioned researching the Ramey clan, her only comment was, "You'd better not go there." Still, isn't making moonshine a distant cousin to wine-making? And how can I ignore the fact that even the French tell me that I look French? And they did— when I was in Paris, at least three French people said if I just learned how to pronounce the French "r" and lost the fanny-pack, I could pass for a *Parisienne*.

Here is another piece of evidence. On my first visit to Paris, a friend and I were lucky to have the free use of an apartment in the Eleventh Arrondissement. We were not so lucky when we broke *la clé* in the front door lock the second day and had to call a locksmith. The *serrurier*, who told us to call him Jérôme, was young and cute and engaged us in flirty conversation while he worked for almost an hour installing a new lock. With such confidence and intellect, he could just as easily have been a commodities trader—but then, French locksmithery has a point of pride: Louis XVI was a frustrated locksmith. Even though he is known primarily for being a bad king, he probably would have been much worse if he hadn't spent the greater part of his twenty-year reign puttering in the castle locksmith workshop.

When Jérôme presented his bill for $300, our eyeballs kind of congealed until he said, *"pas de problème."* I shouldn't have worried— the French have everything figured out, from bread to busted locks. All we had to do, he explained in that adorable accent, was go to the police station, file an attempted burglary report and complete a property damage claim on behalf of the owner, whose insurance would reimburse him. *"Un morceau de gâteau, oui?"* And we did and *oui* it was, plus the young police cadet, Gérard, was also charming. He served us *café* (but no *gateau*) and helped us fill out the forms and wanted to know all about Tennessee . . . well, about Nashville because he was crazy about country music. Of course, we didn't ask the apartment owner to reimburse us since we were staying rent-free, just considered the whole episode a true French experience.

"Jesus!" my husband said on my return home, "They could have pelted you with dog turds, and you would've said, 'My, what a quaint custom.'" *Peu importe.* What is important is that I described the incident in a travel essay and sold it to *France Magazine* for $150, exactly my portion of the bill, which goes to show that I have a bit of what the French prize second only to *liberté, égalité,* and *fraternité,* namely, *naiveté*—ha-ha, just kidding, I mean *suavité* . . . you know, *savoir faire,* the trait the French pride themselves on most and the surest sign that one, even if not born in France, has a *morceau* of French DNA.

But what good is having *savoir faire* if there is no one around who recognizes or appreciates it? It's like having mastered the croissant, but all your friends will eat are biscuits. But *attendez une minute* . . . biscuit is a French word. If something as fundamental as a "biskit" started out French, there must be lots of other Frenchness in Tennessee just waiting to be unbastardized. I decided to reconcile myself to my geography . . . with a *clause conditionelle.* Unlike some who take the easy way and travel to Italy or India or Bali in order to find compatriots and be their best selves, I decided to bring a little of my spiritual home to Tennessee. If America is a melting pot, why not add a pinch of *herbes de Provence* to the homebrew.

So, I began plotting a little *agitation culturelle.* First, I looked for French friends, which was not easy. This is, after all, Tennessee, settled by the Scots, who are incompatible with the French. My first French connection was a woman originally from Ohio. Okay, she wasn't actually French, but she had spent years in France and spoke French fluently and had, *mon dieu,* a bidet. I think it was probably the first (dare I say only?) bidet in Tennessee. She agreed to tutor a group of us psychically displaced Francophiles and started by having us put little stickies with French words on their respective objects throughout the house. Oh, it was *très cher* —everywhere you looked: *la lampe, le lit, la porte, la baignoire.* I started leaving them in restaurants—*la bouteille, le couteau, le moulin de poivre, la toilette des dames.* My husband said Enough! when the waitress at the coffee shop he frequents pulled a sticky from his *postérieur.* Poor guy, he doesn't speak French; how could he know to tell her *la cocotte* meant "casserole dish"?

I bugged the library to order more French films, the coffee shop to carry more dark chocolate, the wine shop to stock more *St. Germain* liqueur. That's the one made from elderflowers handpicked in the French Alps by retired *gendarmes* who carry them in linen bags to the village distillery on *bicyclettes.* When a young girl showed up on a park bench playing French folk tunes on her accordion—a girl who, I swear, looked just like a young *Amélie*—I dropped a five-dollar bill in her basket, her sweet *peu de panier.* My belief is, if one encourages art, one encourages civilization, and where there is civilization, football will soon evolve into soccer, and soccer will attract more French. *Logique, n'est-ce pas?*

My friends and I started wearing berets, and when we parted on street corners, people stared at our flurry of double-cheeked kisses, our high, sing-songy *"bonsoirs," "à bientôts," "à tout à l'heures."* Once, as we were walking into a restaurant, a guy at the bar raised his glass to us and said, *"Ah, la résistance."* Everyone laughed. Me? I was thrilled. Wasn't I indeed part of a resistance? And hadn't I done the impossible, inspired a local to speak French?

Voila! My subversive acts have begun to pay off. Our downtown is attracting more French people. We have a real French restaurant called *Le Parigo* where a real French chef knows what to do with brussels sprouts and how to whip up a *tarte tatin.* We have a *crêperie* called The French Market that orders its flour from France and daily proves the superiority of the *crêpe* over the funnel cake. My favorite organic market, Three Rivers (hmm . . . *Trois-Rivières?*), now stocks fresh *baguettes* and locally produced goat cheese. Like the villages in France, we have a Saturday *marché du fermiers* in the town square where shoppers come with their little baskets and cotton sacks to buy their *legumes organiques* and free-range *oeufs.* Ah, the *bonhomie! L'esprit Français!* Even my mother must be softening to the idea—when I asked her how she liked my new felt cloche, a formless hat created by a Parisian milliner in the Twenties, she laughed and said, "You look like you just came from the Old Country." *Exactement.*

Jo Ann Pantanizopoulos

Xenitiá Redux: 3 nonets

*"When you set out for Ithaca ask that your way be long, full of
adventure, full of discovery . . . ."* —*Ithaca, C.P. Cavafy*

New Mexico is behind me now.
Tumbleweeds scratched against my legs
Making my steps run the course.
Sand carved my crooked way
As I sought more paths
Away from the known
Toward unknown.
Roswell.
Home.
Chicago, Gebenstorf, Athéna
Pittsburg, Jacksonville, Baltimore.
One baby, two, three, and four.
New *xenitiá,* new tongues,
Rich with good stories.
Until one day
Roots need soil.
Knoxville.
Home.
But the itch is still gnawing, pulling
Me to quiet olive groves, naps
With *tzítzika* symphonies
Gauging turquoise shades, hues
Of the Aegean.
Vatopédi
 xenitiá
Comfort.
Home.

xenitiá = foreignness, living in a land of strangers
tzítzika = cicada
Vatopédi = village in the Halkidiki province of northern Greece

Marilyn Kallet

Get This Right

Non, the alderman said, *numéro trois, Place de l'Horloge.*
The Jews used to live near the butcher's,
not the soap shop.   I thanked him.
Need to get this right.

Adéle Kurtzweil tried to study there, before the butchery,
before gendarmes seized her.
Get this right.   Austrian Jews, Bruno, Gisele and their daughter
tried to live in Auvillar—their papers in order.   After Wansee,

the Final Solution, gendarmes grabbed them,
chained off *numéro trois, Place de l'Horloge.*   Fleeing one, two, roundups.
Their papers were in order.
Adele dropped her history book.   Drancy.   Septfois.   Auschwitz.

Not the *savonnerie.*   Right.   I thanked him.
Non, non!   Place of the Clock.

Larry Johnson

Last of the Syrians:

A Guardsman Recalls the Murder of the Emperor Severus Alexander and His Mother at Mainz, March 25, AD 235

The old Augusta had courage, I give her that—
The courage of arrogance, at least. *Ungrateful pigs!*
She shrieked, seizing the emperor's sword. No fat
On her arms or legs, for all her years. Ripe figs
Her favorite meal: we Praetorians all
Had to serve her, but only food, at least once
On palace duty. The contemptible dunce
Who was her son, our sovereign, yet in thrall
To her, retching, tried whimperingly to melt
Into the tent's furred carpet when we felt
It time to act. The keen old harridan then
Swung the blade fiercely, cursing all of us swine
As faithless—flayed slowly and crucified when
Defeated she'd have us, burned fast in resinous pine.

Mark Daniel Compton

Chapter 5 of the Novel *Fruitcake*

Everyone at the wedding knew Lula May's connection to the family and had heard rumors that she was also a root doctor. The congregation ignored her mumblings because of her age, though they did not go unnoticed by Ethel, who watched her closely as if she were going to reveal an old family secret. There were twinkles in Lula May's eyes as she remembered. "It was two years ago on Pearl Harbor Day Miss Bonnie and me went to the Piggly Wiggly like we usually do to buy everything we need to make her fruitcakes."

Bonnie's blue jeans were tight and the fuzzy sweater she wore caught the eyes of bag boys till they got close enough to realize Bonnie was the age of their grandmothers. Before putting her cigarette out in the ashtray provided at the grocery's doors, Bonnie took a deep draw, remembering fondly the days one could smoke anyplace. Lula May, who rarely dressed in store-bought clothes, wore her homemade large floral print dress with matching turban. Each grabbed a cart and made her way into the Piggly Wiggly.

"Miss Lula May, I need a love potion," Bonnie said as bluntly as one could in a whisper.

The two ladies made their way to the produce department. As they spoke, both gathered and placed heaps of candied fruit and nuts in their buggies.

"I thought you said you'd swore off of mens," Lula May said, staring at Bonnie in disapproval.

"It's not for me. It's for Charity." Bonnie said defensively.

"I's sure *she* has, too." Lula May chuckled.

Bonnie replied seriously, realizing the truth in the statement but not appreciating the insinuation. "The way she behaves sometimes I'd think so too, but who knows how long we'll be on this earth, and I don't want her to be alone. My baby Charity needs a man to take care of her."

"And who is it you have in mind for her match?" Lula May said arching her eyebrow like Mr. Spock.

"Why, The Good Reverend Doctor Paul Pruett-Peterson," Bonnie gloated. "He has a steady and honest occupation. He's a widower; he's young enough to still have needs. Now that he is all alone, he needs a strong young woman to help him with that rambunctious son of his, too."

"Yeah, the Good Rev. Dr. Three P's has needs, all right," Lula May said sarcastically under her breath, remembering the story her niece Yvonne had told her a few nights before.

~

Some time ago, Yvonne had worked at the local Texaco station on the outskirts of the black side of town. She was a light-skinned African-American, in her mid-twenties, with green-tipped hair that gave the appearance of a potted Easter lily which had not yet bloomed. Her nails, in which she places great pride (because they are real) were two inches long. As Yvonne was filing her nails, a young man she didn't recognize walked into the gas station store in blue jeans, a sports shirt, and dark sunglasses.

"I'd like some condoms please," the young man had asked.

"I need to see some ID." Yvonne demanded with attitude, not believing some cracker-ass, underage white boy was going to try to buy condoms from her. She looked out the window into a parking lot on the other side of the street, trying to tell if maybe the young man was part of some undercover sting.

"Since when do you need your ID to buy condoms?" the young man questioned, nervously fumbling for his identity.

"Ever since the churches made the city pass its teen-abstinence law — and, Son, my ten-year-old is your height," Yvonne said, staring down at the short man.

He looked outside to his car where a young woman waited. He looked back at Yvonne and took out his ID.

Yvonne looked at it and then laughed. "Take off them sunglasses," she said in disbelief.

He did as she demanded and smiled at Yvonne as his eyes adjusted to the bright fluorescent lights. With the glasses removed, he realized that her hair resembled a green plant and laughed uncontrollably. Both laughed without knowing each other's reason till Yvonne finally got out, "You're forty-five. I'm so sorry, Mister. What kind of condoms do you want? We have Trojans regular and ribbed, with spermacide or without, and Lifestyles Sensitive, small, medium, and large."

"Lifestyles Sensitive, large, please," he said, after collecting himself. With a nod of the head and a matter-of-fact smile, he placed a ten-dollar bill on the counter.

"What God doesn't give us in one area, He compensates for in others." Yvonne said, as if she were testifying in church as she returned his change.

"Amen, Sister, amen," he declared, replacing his sunglasses as he went back to his date with a spring in his step.

Later Yvonne had learned, much to her surprise, that the man was none other than the Reverend Doctor Paul Pruett-Peterson, whose ID had not revealed his calling.

~

Lula May shook the thought from her head and continued shopping. Once they had gathered the needed ingredients, Bonnie and Lula May waited in the check-out line as the grocery's cashier counted out change to the customer in front of them.

"Miss Bonnie, did I ever tell you the story of when my daddy was a sharecropper for your ex-in-laws, the Dicksons, and the time a preacher came to visit while Daddy was working the fields?"

"No, I don't think you have," Bonnie replied.

"Well, I was helping Momma around the house, plucking a chicken as I remembers, when this preacher showed up right out of the blue, so Momma sent me out to fetch Daddy. Well, Honey, it must have been at least a twenty-minute walk to the field Daddy was working in and I told him a preacher had arrived and Momma wanted him to come home right away. Well, there were these storm clouds approaching and Daddy needed to finish work. He said to me, 'Lula May, what kind of preacher is he?' I told him I didn't know. He said to me, 'You go home and you find out. If he's a Holy Roller you put my shine away. If he's a Methodist, you make sure your momma puts aside a nice piece of chicken for me. And if he's Mormon, you set on your momma's lap and don't you get up until I get home.'"

Bonnie laughed out loud. Catching her breath she asked, "Well, which one was he?"

Lula May responded in all seriousness, "He was a Baptist, so I did all three." Bonnie, being Baptist, was offended by the parable and went through the check-out in silence.

While the young bag-boy loaded their groceries into the trunk, Bonnie broke her silence. "The whole family is coming over Friday night to help me with the fruitcakes. I thought I'd pour a little of your love potion on the fruitcake I'm giving to the Rev. Dr. Pruett-Peterson."

Lula May sighed, realizing that her story had not gotten through to Bonnie. "I need her hairbrush, her lipstick, her dirty panties, and whatever liquor you're using, and don't forget to bring some sweet champagne. I'll be calling on Erzulie tomorrow night. She starting to wear me out at my age. Oh, but when I's young, oh, Honey Child, let me tell you what! Ah ha, ooh, child, Erzulie make you hot. You's got to have it. The Rev. Dr. Three-Names will come sniffing for Charity like a dog. All men's dogs. But I warns you, if anyone else gets a hold of that fruitcake with my love potion—anyone, I tells you— they going to fall madly in love with Charity whether she likes it or not."

"Ethel said he ate all of her fruitcake in one setting," Bonnie said still in disbelief. "You know I make the best fruitcake in the county, so he'll eat mine even faster."

The words "best fruitcake in the county" echoed throughout all of Dickson as all the single women in town interested in the widower conversed with their friends over the phone. Even Lula May, who was sometimes hard of hearing, heard the word "county" ringing over and over in her head. Of course, this echo included the voice of Yvonne, who never forgot the name or face of a man who asks for large condoms.

Yvonne walked around her kitchen with a cordless phone glued to her ear, removed the wrappers from a bunch of Claxton fruitcakes, and placed them in a baking pan. She opened a cabinet, took down a quart of brandy, and poured it slowly over the fruitcakes.

"Brenda girl, he's single, makes money and needed the large," she said. Then she sang a parody of "Son of a Preacher Man," changing the words in the chorus to "A Big-Dick Preacher Man."

"And besides, you know I make the best fruitcake in the county," she said with a "Halleluiah!" shaking out the last drop of brandy.

Marianne Worthington

Men at the Mechanic's Wake

These come: soft-handed men in suits,
acquaintances who never smelled
my father's grimed, grease-smeared work clothes.
They talk loud with one another,
shake hands, slap backs like candidates
at the barbeque fundraiser.
They toil at polished desks in cuff-
linked shirts, play golf at private clubs
on lawns of bottle green, float down
the Tennessee in canopied
pontoon boats for football events.

And these: sons of sawmillers,
cattle and tobacco farmers.
The sun has ironed their necks, spotted
their foreheads. Their ropy arms hang
from short-sleeved shirts their wives have pressed

in kitchens smelling of bacon.
They'd rather be in worksheds crammed
with busted machines, paint cans stacked
like pyramids, jelly jars jammed
with tenpennies, sinkers, and bolts
that ground their lives against leaving.

Richard P. Remine
   "Rhea Rural Fair"

KB Ballentine

Old School

He mimics his father, slouching
with thumbs hooked through jeans.
The girl will become her mother,
another unmapped journey. For every
man who reaps his acres, there is
a woman folded, creased within walls,
her route shelved. Even counting
the hens, her visitors are few.

She fuels the stove, fries eggs and bacon,
sends husband and older sons
into the pre-dawn to taste the wind or choke
in its dust. She propels the younger children
across fields, steers their sleepy bodies
to discover a world she no longer misses.

Sun unchains behind the ridge, she boils
water and strips beds, tosses worn sheets
into a kettle to boil away stains. Eyes
searching the hillside, she picks beans
and tomatoes, lays some aside for canning
– bright greens and reds caught, ready
to suspend in row after row of sealed glass.

Her oldest daughter comes over the knoll
with the neighbor boy holding her arm,
one thumb hooked into his jeans.

Joe Rector

Cousins

Edna pulled her chocolate-colored Datsun station wagon into the bottom of the steep driveway. The cover of gravel had been swept away by a series of summer downpours that cut small canyons into the graded ascent. The car door slammed shut in spite of her efforts to hold it open against the slope of her parking spot.

At barely 5'2" she posed little threat. Straight, thick white hair framed her face. Her pale blue eyes peered through a pair of glasses with rims that were ten years out of date. She wore a sleeveless shell and pair of plaid shorts, a wardrobe that was standard except when she exchanged it for work clothes at Dollywood. She'd taken three steps up the drive when the screen door yawned and a man stepped from the house. He wasn't alone; a shotgun accompanied him.

"You need to stop right there," he said.

Edna feared little throughout her sixty years of life, so the warning had little effect on her. "I'm Edna, Edna Balch. Are you Junior?"

"Yep. Who'd you say you was?"

"Edna Balch. Lessie Mae was my mother and Quinton was my daddy." She thought that just identifying herself to Junior would be enough, but his hesitancy continued.

"What brings you out here?"

"You do. I've had you on my mind for a while and figured it was time to reconnect with family. Now, am I coming up, or getting in my car and leaving?

"Awright. Come on up. You alone?

"Yes."

Edna's climb up the driveway left her winded, and she cursed the cigarette habit that had been part of her life long ago. She took the last couple of steps and paused to catch her breath and survey the house, which had clapboard siding in desperate need of a coat of paint. Window sashes rattled with the slam of a door or gusts of wind from the west. Front porch boards were rotten on the ends exposed to the elements. A weathered swing suspended by two rusty chains creaked with the slightest movement. Cane-bottom chairs, items declared valuable antiques in cities, sat in a row against the house, and scuff marks covered the areas where those chair backs had leaned as boys had ridden the seats on two legs. Underneath the porch, a coondog, a beagle and a tabby cat shared the coolness offered by shade and moist ground.

Cousin Junior had undergone great changes over the years since Edna had last seen him. In youth, he was a lean, sinewy boy. A shock of coarse black hair went in half a dozen directions since Junior never ran a comb through it. His arms sported a "farmer's tan," and the parts of his body covered by his shirt were pale as the moonlight and covered with a bountiful crop of freckles.

Now he was a larger individual. In fact, he would field-dress at about 300 pounds. His everyday wardrobe consisted of T-shirts with yellow sweat stains around the neck and armpits and bib overalls made with enough material to sew up a tent. His hair had raced to the crown, and a ball cap covered the bald head to prevent sunburn.

Edna and her family had moved from Parrotsville years earlier, but not before she'd been named valedictorian of her high school class. She worked summers at the Stokely factory to earn enough money for a class ring. She earned a two-year teaching certificate, but by the time she'd married, had three children, and applied for a teaching position, a bachelor's degree was required. For the next ten years she took classes at night and during summers to graduate. Knoxville became home, but she loved travel and journeyed to Europe, Canada, and most of the states.

Junior didn't cotton much to school. It took time away from the things he liked—hunting, fishing, and sleeping. Work was a profane four-letter word to him, and as he aged, his dislike for labor grew. The man never held a steady job in his life, at least not the legal kind. He learned his trade in the dense foliage of East Tennessee. With other natives of Cocke County, he set up camp and stirred a witches' brew that revenuers had vowed for a generation to destroy. Junior was an honor student like Edna, but his course of study focused mainly on chemistry and cooking. As a young man he learned how to mix liquids and cook corn mash. He also learned marketing logistics as his products were bottled and distributed to thirsty customers in all areas of East Tennessee, as well as southern Kentucky and Virginia.

Junior was still uneasy with this stranger's visit. He and Edna had been close as children; they played in yards together, and with a slew of kids, they trekked down to the creek and waded or sat on a fallen tree across it and talked as their feet kicked the water. Their families shared meals and celebrated holidays together.

Their paths diverged in high school, and with each year the distance increased. Education was important to Edna's parents. Her dad worked on a dairy farm; he rose at 4:30 a.m. to milk cows and spent the rest of the day doing back-breaking work. In the evenings after supper, he sat in his favorite chair, slung one of his lanky legs across the chair arm, and read until midnight. Her mother read as well, although her literature choice was the King James Bible. Her three brothers also became readers.

Edna learned that love of reading early in life and developed it by reading late into the night. Her parents threatened her with spankings if she didn't go to bed, so she would sneak a flashlight under the covers to finish book after book.

Such activities were frowned on by people in the hills and dells of Cocke County. They labeled such activities as "triflin'" because they led to no tangible result. Junior never cared a whit about reading. He got along fine without it and used the skill only to learn how to mix up ingredients when he first started making liquor. Before long he had the recipe memorized and again spurned reading.

Other relatives held the same low opinion of reading and writing. They allowed only enough education to soak in to enable them to sign their names and count to one hundred. Filling their heads with any more crowded out more important things like carpentry skills, farming information, and community gossip. Life in Cocke County was dominated by manual labor that scratched out a living for families.

Of course, some relatives managed to escape. They were Edna's paternal kin. Her dad's two brothers packed up and left as soon as possible. One finished his college education and spent years as a high school Latin teacher in North Carolina. His children and grandchildren treasured education. They chose lives as college professors, chefs, and doctors. The entrepreneurial spirit like that present in Junior also flowed through their veins. One grandson established a business in Alaska as a guide, but he did so only after earning a degree from an Ivy League university.

The other brother earned his degree in civil engineering and spent his working years with the Tennessee Valley Authority building dams. He settled in Nashville with his family. One son became a Methodist minister and counselor.

The cousins sat on the front porch the rest of the afternoon and recalled the good things they could remember from childhood. Junior's tongue loosened, and before long he was engaged in long, descriptive tales of years gone by. Edna remained silent even though she knew her kin's memories were colored with the tint of what could have been, instead of what had been. It was all right because what she craved most was reconnecting with family who lived at the base of the Smoky Mountains. They were of the same bloodline, but what each considered important in life separated them as much as the Great Smoky Mountains did Tennessee and North Carolina.

Edna pulled herself from the porch swing and announced she needed to head toward home. Junior sat quiet for a minute and then said, "Think you'll come back sometime?"

"If it's all right with you, I'll make it a regular thing."

"That'll be awright, I reckon."

She walked toward her cousin and put her arms half-way around him—that's as far as they reached. "It's good to see you again. Family ought to stay in touch, no matter how far apart they live or how different their lives are."

"I reckon we both might need t'do better."

Edna descended the driveway to the car. She drove in the twilight of the evening and thought about how different folks can be. Then she said a prayer of thanks for her parents and the things she'd been taught. Was that life better? No. It was different, and it suited her. She added to the prayer by thanking the good Lord for the many paths that are available to His children.

Damaris Victoria Kryah

The Lady of the Dahlias

As I drove down the highway, the slanting sunlight became a mirror of memory for another autumn day when the sky was the same intense blue. White clouds moved through the blue then, the sun hanging low, inviting the maples to flame before winter. I watched milkweed seed blowing across endless fields of gray corn stalks. I turned the car onto a dirt road, drawn by the light fragmenting the ragged husks. Stopping beside one of the fields, I stepped out into chest-high clumps of purple ironweed. They tempted me to take their portraits as I retrieved my camera bag from the trunk, but I was drawn to the fields. I walked through the rows of dried corn, photographing these patterns of light, trying to capture them on film. I followed the light until I was lying on my back, shooting straight up at the blue spilling through Matisse-like cutouts.

Lost in the camera's images, I didn't see the tractor but heard its slow approach across the fields. The farmer turned off the engine, answering my questions in the easy, friendly way of most East Tennessee farmers who enjoy a conversation with a stranger. "Yes, all these fields, several hundred acres, belong to me. Well, me and my sister Pearl. Take all the pictures you want." From his high vantage, he pointed in the direction of an old house bordered by fields on three sides. "Pearl don't get out much. She lives up yonder in our folks' old homestead. You can't dynamite Pearly out of Ma's old house. Most days she just sets all alone. I sure would be obliged if you'd pay her a visit. I got to get back to my fields. I'm behind this year. Fact is, I stay behind."

I followed his gaze toward the house. It stood sturdy and plain, well proportioned. Its windows looked out on the road and the small front yard. Black shutters like sentinels contrasted with the lace curtains inside. The white clapboards were permanently steeped in autumn melancholy. As I turned away, I glimpsed a garden alongside the house that fed my artist's eye. From the distance, it was more colorful than the surrounding foliage. I walked the field toward the house, breathing in the smell of musty leaves, smoke and damp clay. I crossed the boundary between plowed field and yard to climb the steps of the porch.

~

Pearl sat in the dim light of the house's front room, the familiar place with the faded wallpaper and the worn pine floor with the cracks between the boards, the same cracks she had stood her homemade paper dolls in. Faintly she heard the tractor bumping across the fields. She stood up, pulled back the curtain, peering to see if it was Clarence, her heart expanding with a joy she seldom felt for another human. He was driving in the direction of a woman bent in the corn field, holding a camera. Most people seemed strange to Pearl, but this woman particularly so because of the camera. She dropped the curtain, letting it cover the window, as if she had veiled her face and could look at the world hidden. Afraid of being seen, yet wanting Clarence to come visit, she sat back down in the chair that had held her since childhood; worn and stiff, it matched her own body. Her hands plucked and smoothed the fabric that covered the chair. Pearl heard the footsteps and the knock on the door, but she was lost in the place where the hinge of memory had come loose.

~

I knocked on the front door but no one came. There had been a face at the window; surely Pearl was home. I heard the lock turning, then the heavy door opened to reveal a woman. She stood before me white-haired and wind-blown. The interior of the house was dark. No cat came curling a furry anklet around her feet. She was alone and had sifted down life's uncertainties to a few; a stranger knocking on her door was one of them. She hesitated, as if she had lost the capacity to endure an encounter with a stranger. To reassure her, I spoke quietly, "Your brother Clarence sent me."

Her arms crossed protectively, puffy fingers fluttered at her shoulders. "I don't get much company," she said, hooding her eyes from scrutiny. Her vacant way of speaking made her seem insubstantial. Torn between apprehension and curiosity, she stepped through the door, surprising herself like a small child who lets go of its parent's hand and remains standing.

The front door opened to the porch, down the walk and to the road. "I promised Clarence I wouldn't go near the road," she said. Trying to hide her anxiety, she jammed her fingers in her pockets, but they rose to her breast again. Her fingernails were tiny black crescents against the floral print of her dress.

"Are you a gardener?" I asked.

She seemed empty, anonymous, reluctant to inflict herself on me. Suddenly her eyes opened. I gazed back directly, unflinching. She was startled at being so quickly spun into existence; a flower pressed in a forgotten book, she slipped from the page when opened. Her glance held something elusive. It slept under her eyelids, in the liminal space between what was dream and what was real, that place where two people meet out of context. I experienced a reverent respect between us, much like what the Greeks called *aidos*. In answer to my question, she looked straight at me, her head moving slightly up and down.

"Are *you* a gardener?"

When I answered "Yes," she grabbed my hand. "I'd be pleased to show you my garden." Her eyes, wide and vulnerable, were beseeching in an innocent way.

"My name's Pearl."

"My name is Victoria."

Averting her gaze from the road, she held my hand tighter as we maneuvered the porch steps. "I don't never go to the garden from

here," she whispered, leading me in the opposite direction to the back
of the house. When we reached the kitchen door, she followed a narrow,
worn path. She was careful not to wander onto the grass on either side;
side paths were not part of Pearl's life. Even in the dark of a moonless
night, this path, familiar and comfortable, guided her to the garden. As
we walked, voices and images seemed to accompany us.

*"Pearly, you hold Miss Trula's hand when you take her out to see the
garden. I swear, Trula, I think Pearl loves those flowers more than me. You two
go on now. I'll just finish up these dumplins and shell the peas. I'll get out my
new tablecloth and when you come back, Pearly, you can set the table. Cut
some flowers but Lordy, Pearl, be careful with them scissors. And Pearly
Bohanan, you better not step off that path. Miss Trula, you be sure Pearl don't
lead you astray. She don't have enough sense to find her way back to the house,
even in her own yard."*

Pearl opened the gate. Together the two of us turned the corner,
where we found ourselves cloistered in flowers. The garden had been
waiting expectantly, filled with dahlias in full bloom, their petals
opening against the blunted days of the house. Pearl's random pattern
of planting had created a labyrinth of saturated color and dancing
forms. We stood in this jewel box of spangled light, filling our eyes with
red, violet, tangerine and Chinese yellow. It felt like I had been given
Kandinsky's gift of not only seeing color but hearing and feeling it as
well. I stood still, experiencing the dance of the changing brightness, the
flowers and this gardener. Pearl turned slowly, almost majestically, to
look at me, to see if the garden's magic was doing its work. She met my
gaze, eyes focused, a smile softening the lines of her face. The faint
scent of rain swept through the garden like a foggy whisper.

*"Wake up Clarence! Wake up! Pearly's gone missing again and I ain't
about to wake your Pa up at this hour. Hurry! Take the lantern and find her."
Clarence always found her huddled in the garden, her lap full of flowers,
talking to them as if they were human. All her night terrors were absorbed in
the garden, as if the flowers dispelled her darkness. Here the past did not pierce*

her memory, forcing her into selves she could no longer inhabit. She looked up, surprised to see Clarence looking down at her. "Pearly, you ain't got good sense, going out in such a night as this. You worry Ma to death." He reached down for her hand. Calmed after sitting in the garden, she would allow him to lead her, rain-soaked, back to the house.

Pearl walked among the dahlias touching each one, speaking some language encoded in her being. She was a balm of regeneration for each dahlia. There was no separation between Pearl and the flowers; boundaries dissolved in a radiant transference. She bent over the small ones, cupping her hands gently around each blossom as if she were holding the face of some beloved child. They imperceptibly turned towards her, the way sunflowers turn toward the sun. The tall ones brushed against her, so tall they touched her face as she passed, swaying to her rhythm in some magical symphony of light and color. Where did this blooming come from, teaching her to believe in herself?

Misunderstood in this place where everyone knows their identity and purpose, she had fashioned what could almost be called a self. Whom did Pearl toil for? Certainly not a husband, nor children, not even the narrow life of the community. Could one devote a life to a flower? Before Pearl, the garden did not exist. Before the garden, neither did Pearl. As she dug in the earth, her physical senses returned. Together they wove a pattern in the dahlias' cycles. Sharing rejuvenation, they each gave of their beauty, compassion and patience. In the garden the break with the world, with herself, was mended.

Her fingers stiff from the chill air, Pearl dug a handful of cold tubers. Carefully, using a pair of rusty scissors tied to the gatepost, she snipped off the dead flower heads. She knew flowers reached a time when they began to droop, smelling of grief. It was this smell that drove her into the house as winter approached. With the dirt still clinging to them, she thrust them awkwardly towards me.

I reached out for the delicate dahlias, knowing they required a great deal of care. Pearl, without faltering, gave instructions on their cultivation. "They must be dug in the late fall and stored in a dark, cool place, but not where they might freeze. When warm weather returns and all danger of frost has passed, the tubers are planted again. Dig a hole twelve inches deep and fill with compost and some bonemeal. Lay the tuber longways about six inches down with the eye pointing up."

I listened attentively, aware that her voice had faded as she finished giving the instructions. I didn't thank her because in this part of the world, some gardeners believe the plants won't grow if one thanks the giver.

My arms filled with dahlias, I followed her, a Venus of Willendorf in house slippers and a cotton dress the wind flattened against her thighs. She led me through the front yard, looking behind her at the bent blades of a delicate trail from the garden. She had made her own path. As the garden's protective boundaries receded, Pearl became anxious. Disoriented, she turned toward the road, then stopped and faced the house, climbing the porch steps.

The setting sun had gilded the wavy windowpanes to mirrors. Perceiving herself, she paused as if reading her own story. Then she looked at my image. "Please call on me again." I couldn't answer because I had glimpsed beyond the glass into the dark house. Pearl waved her hand, as if she could scatter the reflection. Then she stepped inside, closing the front door behind her. There was no turning of the lock, only silence.

I crossed the field, stopping to look back. The perspective of distance gave me the photograph I had been searching for. Divested of detail, the house was a silhouette the color of Parma violets. The approaching dark had quenched the fire of the sunset, diffusing the colors of garden and sky into a glow of muted lavenders shot with molten gold. Absorbed in watching the twilight, I could not lay down the dahlias and shoot. Pearl and the dahlias seemed to dissolve, only to reconstruct and dissolve again.

I drove down the road several years later. The windows of the house were shuttered tight against the view of chain link. Was the fence there to keep Pearl enclosed, or the world out? As I stood there looking at the cold dirt of the abandoned garden, it felt sacred. Exactly why, I could not answer. The dahlias had claimed Pearl in the iridescence of a thousand petals across the valley.

In the chill, a lone writing spider worked her web between house and garden. I watched, my lips pressed tight. When I was a child, I believed if I smiled, showing my teeth, the writing spider would write my name on her web and I would be lost forever.

Connie Jordan Green

Song of the Farmer

Late September, season's last cutting,
hay falls behind the mower
like pale sheets billowed over a bed.
Dry weather crisps the grass
so baler can do its work—
cut, pack, tie square packages
we load onto a wagon, haul
to barn loft where we build
a fort against winter's hunger.
Come January's cold, we'll feed
the stock—horses huddled
in barn's lee, cows on a hillside,
faces toward the weather—
scatter the gold we collect
this day, remember sun's
warm hand, smell of dryness,
remember how it feels
to have too much.

Elizabeth Howard

Bean Fields

Grant Asbury rubs his hand, the aching stub.
He dreamed about the accident again last night,
the chainsaw leaping from the knothole—
pain, blood, hospital. He woke up sweating.
Couldn't go back to sleep, remembered pain
as fresh as the first pain twenty years ago.

On a perfect day like this, a man
middle-aged and strong as an ox
ought to be in the fields, an example
to his sons and hired hands (if he had any),
but here he sits on the tailgate of his pickup
watching Haitians pick his beans.
The Haitians, beautiful people,
clad in broad hats and brilliant clothes,
like patches of flowers—red, blue, pink,
yellow—blooming in the green fields.
Regal, the word that comes to his mind
when he sees them standing in the shed lot,
walking to buses, bending over rows,
toting crates on their shoulders.
No quit in any of them, men or women.

His sons escaped the bean fields early,
took city jobs as bankers and lawyers;
the hired hands fled to factories or construction.
But his young grandson rushes to the fields
after school, works alongside the Haitians,

talks to them, tries to speak their language,
says it's nothing like his high school French.
Who knows what the future holds for these fields.
Will his grandson be part of it?
Will the Haitians? For now, he is content.
Laughter rising from a field is fine music.

Dick Penner

"Reflecting Man"

Jack Rentfro

Nothing Makes Any Sense

If my years at the University of Tennessee in Knoxville taught me anything, it was that the important things are learned outside the classroom—something my parents, footing the bill for me since private high school, would have appreciated.

It was the early '70s. The Vietnam war was still on. The conscription sweepstakes to fight in America's most unpopular war was instituted my freshman year. So, yeah, I felt some passions about the war. It was easy when you had just drawn a safe lottery number—284 out of a possible 365.

After receiving that bit of federal correspondence, my anticipation of seeing the frozen North by way of the trans-Canadian railway like local hero and folk-rocker Jesse Winchester subsided.

Even though it was actually the early '70s, the South was, culturally speaking, as with nearly everything, behind the curve. The rage that came and went with the '60s passed through even quicker in the South. I had cheered when anti-war elements vandalized UT's Reserve Officer Training Corps offices, but I was militarist enough to idolize the older men in my family who had served, one having been posted with the Marines at Quang Tri, supporting the garrison at Khe Sanh. Just weeks after National Guardsmen murdered students at a Kent State war protest, President Nixon spoke in Knoxville with Billy Graham. All that went down more than a year before I came to UT. It's not like we never rioted. But by 1971, big street scenes in Knoxville likely had something to do with Alabama weekend. Of course, there was also that boisterous crowd demanding co-ed dormitories ("2-4-6-8/We wanna cohabitate"). The closest I ever came to the legendary clique of protesters known as the Knoxville 22 who had jeered the Graham-Nixon visit was when I learned my religion professor was one of them.

After the mining of Haiphong Harbor and the clandestine incursion across the Cambodian border's so-called "Parrott's Beak," there wasn't much to protest except girls not sleeping with us. Sometimes this was made easier through the application of "Guerrilla Biscuits," better known as Quaaludes, basically a 50-cent license for any kind of behavior imaginable. But the drug scene was as slack as our '70s generation's political conscience. Operation Aquarius, the great drug crackdown that resulted in the suspension of Constitutional rights for unlucky souls, very few of whom were truly guilty, was wrapping up. Many of my peers and I believed that the city's safety director, Randy Tyree, whose exploitation of that omnibus police job description cinched his political future, had dreamed up most of Operation Aquarius' good and bad guys out of thin air.

I was actually more concerned with how the war's progress seemed to parallel the long campaign to lose my virginity. There was a slow buildup, just advisors at first, escalating from high school posturings and the siege at Khe Sanh and concluding with the attainment of various technical achievements between the Tet Offensive and Vietnamization. To me, "Peace with Honor" could be a bad pun as well as an oxymoron.

That would describe my political and hormonal orientation as I came to the big city from the lily-white enclave where I grew up a couple of hours' drive south of Knoxville. Maybe I would have been ready to take my position at the barricades if anything had been going on. But I had come to a campus where there was precious little activism to fire my indignation. My peers and I discovered that the new mission was to party. Why else would Winfield Dunn, a conservative who would be Tennessee's first Republican governor in half a century, have lowered the drinking age from 21 to 18 the very year I turned 18? This was what the Cosmos intended. Seeing it any other way wouldn't make sense. Thus was I morally cleared to concentrate on the new mandate: when nothing else makes sense, party.

Convinced of my role as special envoy from the New—liberal— South and pretty much leaving a trail of testosterone, I quickly caught on to the social value of being a bellbottomed boulevardier on The Strip. The Strip was the section of Cumberland Avenue—part of old Knoxville's road west—that had become a Casbah of sorts, a marketplace between the actual campus and the funky old Fort Sanders neighborhood where the "adult" students lived. The alleys, bars and shops of the Strip would be the classrooms of my second coming of age, my firebases for all future illegal border activities. I learned how to triage the casualties in the war against conformity. I learned the lore and the lingo and was well on my way to becoming a stereotype. It would be a very long time before I learned how little I knew.

Just as progressives of the era could congratulate themselves that the Civil Rights struggle had ended in triumph, a historic event popped up like a latent pimple on a teenager who thought he'd grown past that. The Indians wanted to be heard.

Remember the party I mentioned? It was sound-tracked by WROL, Knoxville's first "album oriented rock" [AOR] station. The deejays were the coolest of all time—actually taking bong hits on the air. In the context of the paranoia triggered by Operation Aquarius, it was revolutionary—"heads" blowing minds while feeding us whole LPs of Frank Zappa, Bob Dylan, Pink Floyd, Jimi Hendrix, the Rolling Stones, the Beatles—especially "The White Album"—and everything after. Unfettered by the demands of the commercial singles format, AOR brought different styles of radio patter. It was important to some deejays that we knew they were getting high.

The bubbling and inhaling sounds added another layer of stick-it-to-the-Man righteousness when the deejays tried to rally Fort Sanders on the night of the FBI's surrender deadline for radical members of the American Indian Movement. AIM militants were holed up in a protest at Wounded Knee in South Dakota, a place sanctified by the slaughter of Sioux shamans called "Ghost Dancers" and other innocent tribespeople by U.S. troops a little less than a century earlier.

Nobody knew exactly what we were supposed to do about an armed standoff a thousand miles away. We didn't even know of a substantial Native American presence in East Tennessee with whom to show solidarity. We weren't aware of any local Native protests in East Tennessee since Andrew Jackson's soldiers forced the exodus of the Cherokee. There wasn't a shout-out from the Eastern band. Those

Cherokee on the North Carolina side of the state line may have ducked out on the Trail of Tears, but these days, they were best known to most of us for abjectly dancing on the side of the road for tourist dollars.

That night shift, the deejays at WROL—"Real Rock and Roll Radio"—played every song they could that smacked remotely of Native American culture: anything performed by anyone with Indian roots, like Rita Coolidge and Buffy Sainte-Marie. The countdown even sank to the level of Paul Revere and the Raiders' cheesy masterpiece "Cherokee Nation."

Midnight came, as did the end of that 71-day siege in South Dakota in early 1973. The AIM members lay down their weapons and filed out of their stronghold, arms overhead, in surrender. During the course of the confrontation, several federal agents and Sioux were killed. The arrest of AIM leader Leonard Peltier would be a source of controversy to the present day.

In just another few years after Wounded Knee, Tennessee Valley Authority cited eminent domain and evicted the poor whites who had settled in the valley of the Little Tennessee River, whose river bottoms were rich with burials and remnants of the Cherokee civilization—all in favor of rich whites who wanted a magnificent lakefront to develop. About a century and a half had passed since the Cherokee had been driven out of the Little Tennessee's fertile valley and the rest of their tribal lands at bayonet-point.

WROL became a disco station a year or two after the Second "battle" of Wounded Knee, but there were plenty of Ghost Dancers to keep the party going. Every year or so, when Knoxville hosts a "powwow," it seems the native people of the Americas are represented mainly by blond, dread-locked kids. It makes me think of those deejays wringing counter-cultural melodrama out of Wounded Knee.

The years of one's youth should be eye-opening. You are supposed to take all that excess and callow adventuring and distill wisdom from it. If that is the warrior's path, I like to think I followed it with at least middling success. Looking back from a middle age that seems far less settled and certain than it did for the parents in the sitcoms that baby-sat me, the only thing I'm sure of is a remarkable synchronicity limning it all—a curious overlay to events that superficially seem disconnected. Like the fact that the chief FBI investigator at Wounded Knee, Norman Zigrossi, moved to Knoxville to become TVA's inspector general—which proves history is not just a continuum, it's a Moebius strip, forever turning in on itself.

We need circumstances to have meaning, to be guided by an objective, omniscient power. But, if that were the case, couldn't this—let's call it "Great Spirit"—at least let life make sense?

One of the most visible Native Americans in this part of the world these days does a good job of marginalizing himself with no help from the government. In fact, he wants to be part of the government. Perennial gubernatorial candidate Carl "Two Feathers" Whitaker is about my age. Presumably, he witnessed the same history that I watched unfold. Yet he arrives at this point in time with different conclusions. He is an American Indian with devout Tea-Party leanings—perhaps most poignantly his support for stronger immigration laws—and proud membership in separatist neo-Confederate organizations. A paralegal in Sevierville, the Cherokee-Mohican (detractors question his true heritage) is a founder of a group that echoes that old radical group of the '70s in name only—the Native American Indian Movement. Admirably, NAIM advocates protection of Indian burial sites.

Arguably, the only unassimilated Indians in Knoxville are some of the other Cherokee who dodged Jackson's roundup—the ones in the shoeboxes full of bones exhumed by UT archaeologists before the impoundment of the Little Tennessee River into Tellico Lake, whose removal from the soon-to-be-flooded river plain would no doubt have been opposed by Whitaker's group. Now those cartons are stacked in academic catacombs beneath Neyland Stadium where the cheering of crowds drowns out a world that won't end no matter how badly we behave.

Whitaker came in third in 2010, getting the most votes of any independent (0.41 percent, or 0.0041, of the vote) after the race's Democratic and Republican Party big shots. But if you click on his website to read his views, you are directed to pages of Kanji script for some Japanese Internet concern.

I can't help but wonder what Whitaker—if he is a genuine Native American sincerely protesting the arrival of illegals from Hispanic countries—thinks of the white men yelling alongside him. As for me, in spite of my privileged white Southern background—or perhaps because of it—I encourage all manner of folk to come live in this most perfect expression of nationhood and stand in the same lines with me. Maybe they'll have something good to say to make time go by pleasantly.

I still don't think anything makes sense. And maybe it's too late to party, but we can still learn something.

Penny L. Wallace

"Knights of the Roundtable"

Andre Canty

The Mic

"I don't care about any of those rappers."

Yes, Skyner "Sky" Davis did not concern himself with any competitors. The rappers he referred to were several rivals who wanted to take his throne. Sky Davis, named after the fictitious Michael Jordan-esque character from the 1990s cartoon "Doug," was the first rapper from Knoxville, Tennessee, to get a major publishing deal.

The day Skyner arrived at Knoxville's only rap and R&B radio station to address all detractors and haters, who had increased in number since his signing, he declined an introduction.

"Let me spit." *Spitting* was a synonym for rapping. Sky Davis wanted to speak in rhyme exactly what was on his mind.

He grabbed the microphone as if he owned it. A rap about guns, drugs, women, and a call for the death of all of his opponents came out of his mouth without a piece of paper to read from. This was called a "freestyle rap," in which one rapped over a random instrumental and the rhymes were all improvised.

Sky's rap voice was the antithesis of his actual voice. His regular speech, though slang-ridden, was spoken with correct pronunciation. When he came into the station, the DJ mentioned the time they had spent together when they were theatre students in college, but playing the lead in a local rendition of the musical *Cats* at the Bijou Theatre wasn't exactly gangsta. Sky knew if anyone discovered this secret from his past, his rap career and his card-carrying status as a heterosexual African-American male would be compromised.

"Yo, I don't know what you talking about. I don't do sucka stuff," Sky said. He told the DJ as quietly as he could to keep that portion of his life in the closet.

Sky was dressed in "Street Prep": an oversized hoodie over a baseball cap, a sweater vest and size 29x29 jeans, despite his actual pants size of 35x34. You could see the outline of his thighs.

Pushing his curled lips close to the microphone, Sky said, "Nah, man. These cats think that I'm supposed to sit back and take this hate on me? I got the number one record on the radio right now and got two, yeah I said it, *two* record deals. Marinate on that!"

Sky's warning to competitors was followed by computer-simulated gunshots, followed by further simulated gunshots from Sky's mouth. "*Blacka, blacka, blacka.* That's all you gonna hear when you step up to me! I'm tired of you cats thinking you can take the throne."

The DJ read off some emails from listeners regarding the rivalry between Sky and a former member of his crew called White Line, whose real name was Calvin Coolidge (not that one). White Line had christened Sky as a traitor because he hadn't brought him or his crew into his one-million-dollar five-disc deal. Then, White Line himself called in.

"Negro, you wrote that rhyme back in the day. You fake, bruh. Your girl told me so!" White Line's cell phone sputtered in and out. "You is . . . fool . . . ole Benedict Arnold . . . Judas . . . and your baby mama want the steel . . . and I don't mean my 9mm."

"What about *your* baby mama?" Sky responded. "That girl has been running the streets at night for the longest time. Peanut, Pookie, Slim, and Ty-Man all been with her!"

What the listening audience didn't know was that Sky and White Line had been friends since high school. Their freestyle battles were legendary in the school cafeteria.

"Yeah, man," Skyner retorted. "I suggest you stay back before you get pushed back. I can only hold your hand for so long. I changed your diapers and fed you."

"And I let you wear my clothes," White Line huffed.

"I bailed you outta jail," Sky countered.

"You owed me that."

"I gave you rides."

"Yeah, off the car we both put money in when we worked at KFC."

Now White Line got mad for real. "You are fake, homeboy. Before you got big you were talking about more relevant things. You used to talk about how bad things were in the 'hood. Remember that one song when you talked about the death of that little girl and how it got the police to arrest her killer? It's all about the drug game now. You lost your soul, brotha."

Sky fidgeted in his chair. It was true. Two years before he signed his contract, he wrote a dedication rap for a teenage girl who was raped and killed by her stepfather in a back alley off Martin Luther King, Jr. Avenue, a street known for crimes that were the antithesis of its namesake. Finally the song gained enough attention to put pressure on the Knoxville Police Department to investigate.

"Hang up on this fool," Sky demanded.

The DJ could not bring himself to do what Sky wanted. This broadcast was the most listened to in the show's short history.

"Don't you hang up on me, homeboy. I still got plenty to say."

"Say what?" Sky demanded. "Didn't I pay your light bill with our show money and put you in a nice apartment after your house voucher expired? You know where I'm at. Come see me. I'll beat that behind like your mama should've. Start with one of your four guts. You know you have a stomach like a cow. If you win, then you get my chain. It cost more than your yearly salary."

There was a two-second silence from White Line. Then his mouth made the sound of a gun clicking. "Meet me outside the station then. My house is up the street from there. You know what my car look like."

When Sky leaped up, most of the station's staff followed him. Listeners from the nearby area walked up to the station for first-hand observation of the fight. One of the engineers carried a laptop with a Webcam, so he could document the confrontation between the two rival rappers and put it on YouTube and all the rap blog sites.

The cold air was tearing Sky's eyes. He saw his baby mama pushing through the crowd to get to him. "Baby, I don't really want to do this," he whispered in her ear.

"You got this, Sky. Don't let that fool get to you. Make him eat your K-Swiss." K-Swiss shoes were popular at the time.

"Who still wears K-Swiss?" asked one spectator. No response.

When the blue Chevy Caprice pulled into the parking lot, Sky recognized the car he gave to White Line after their graduation. The irony of the situation was not lost on him. He remembered the time he took White Line to step-shows, football games, and all things college to share his experience with his friend. Reconciliation was on his mind.

Sky knocked on the car's tinted window. There was no response, so he bent down, trying to peer inside. The window was cracked open enough for him to speak.

"This is stupid, bruh," he shouted. "We are better than this. Come on. Let's just play this off like we fighting." Skyner also told the DJ to edit that part out and only broadcast the pretend fight.

When the window finally did roll down, Sky smiled at the person behind the wheel.

Blacka, blacka, blacka! This time the gunshots were real, not simulated.

"Oh my God! No! No!"

"Bruh, get his chain!" someone yelled.

"Oh my God! Oh my God!" Sky's woman dropped to the ground. "Sky's been shot. Call the cops!"

The DJ held up his hand. "Wait!" he shouted. "Everybody listen up! White Line is still on the phone. His younger brother Eli took his car. He heard the riff on the radio and thought it was for real. White Line tried to make him understand it was all a fake, a set-up to make the two look badass, but Eli wouldn't listen."

"Oh my God!"

After the ambulance left, the crowd started to disperse.

Sky Davis wanted to taste the fame shared by numerous rappers before him. He tried to follow the formula used by modern rappers through the art of an overhyped and manufactured conflict. He wanted to be the king of the rap game, the gatekeeper of the culture's movement, but all he was now was dead.

Calls flooded the radio station with conspiracy theories, from Sky Davis' death being faked to his eventual return with Tupac Shakur. There was no funeral, just a block party in the 'hood. White Line took Sky's old rap songs and sold them as a "lost tapes" album. Ironically, death was Sky Davis' biggest career move.

Peggy Douglas

Same Difference

I couldn't be like her, Mama—perky, sultry,
on the cover of *TV Guide.* I went the other way
from Doris Day. Ended up in Berkeley with foggy
nights and a lover who threw bricks at cop cars.

We walked midnight streets on psychedelics,
measuring time by fading colors, cooked
dinner in the morning—pinto beans in a pot
on a two-burner stove, never talked of marriage
and children. Sometimes, I peeled the curtain
from the steamy kitchen window as the sun rose
and pictured the *TV Guide* in your hands.

So I called you Sunday, across three time zones
to breathe affection through the gaps in our bones.
Me, in a dirty phone booth sipping Boone's Farm
from a jelly glass on Haight Street, one hand pressed
against the free ear so I wouldn't miss a single word,
while you left your Sunday dishes to soak
until they got cold.

Lauren Hutchins

Sweet Sloppy Kisses

Six a.m. wake up,
With a sweet sloppy kiss.
Three smiley-face pancakes,
Chocolate milk just for Sis.

Shoes to be tied,
Lunches to make.
"Honey, on your way home,
Will you pick up the cake?"

Drop off at school,
Head to the store.
Juice boxes and popsicles,
Do we need three apples or four?

Home to do laundry,
Whites, colors, and darks.
Never-ending piles,
"Mommy, can we go to the park?"

Picnic at the park,
Bread for the ducks.
Baby needs a nap,
Long walk back to the truck.

Wake up the baby,
Here come the tears.
"Sweetheart, don't cry!"
Must find his Teddy Bear!

Late to pick up Sis,
Now another grouchy kid.
Bottle of water and aspirin,
Took two, glad I did.

Spaghetti for dinner,
Whose turn to wash dishes?
Homework and baths,
Feed the dog and the fishes.

Bedtime, my angels,
Finally alone with Dad.
Tiny knock on the door,
"Mommy, I need you, real bad!"

At last, snuggle in bed,
Drift to sleep in serene bliss.
Tomorrow will begin like today,
With a sweet sloppy kiss.

Aaron DiMunno

Scooby-Doo for Dinner

I'm screaming "Mommy!" with everything I've got as I come tearing into the kitchen, slide to a stop across the linoleum and pull on my mother to come back with me into the flickering blue living room. "Scooby saw a monster!"

I'm four.

"Aaron, I'm trying to get dinner ready!"

Mom yells over her shoulder at me from the sizzling stovetop. She's wearing a blue paisley bandana around her head. It reminds me of Aunt Jemima from the syrup bottle. Every afternoon during the Scooby-Doo cartoons Mom is in the kitchen.

My dad is a carpenter. He comes home grumpy most nights smelling like sawdust and sweat and he wants his dinner.

Mom has figured out a great way to buy herself some time when dinner isn't started and Dad is on his way home. She puts a pan on the stove, chops up some onions and garlic with a little bit of butter, and chooses low to medium flame proportional to the imminence of my father's ill-tempered arrival; within minutes the house is bursting with the aroma of a cooking meal. Scooby-Doo and the savory smell of grilling garlic and onions remain inextricable in my memory.

I return sullen to the sofa in front of the television. The Scooby gang is at a farm investigating a stolen chicken fricassee recipe. I have to bury my face in the cushions just to make it to the end of the episode.

"Okay, dinner's in the oven. Daddy's late for dinner again." My mom is wiping her hands on a dish towel in the doorway to the kitchen. "Let's get you in the bath."

I hate taking baths. I hate the shampoo in my eyes. I want to play with my boats but my mom always wants to scrub my arms or wiggle the wash cloth in my ears. So I run.

"Aaron! Come on, Mommy doesn't need this right now. Upstairs! Let's go!"

144

I am too young to question why a carpenter has to work after dark. I think it's a game. It's fun to make mom chase me.

Mom isn't in the mood, but she doesn't yell. She hatches a plan.

"Hey! I know! Why don't we invite Scooby and those guys over for dinner?" Just like that. As if she were inviting my playmate Eric or the neighbors across the street.

"What?" I freeze in my tracks on the dining room carpet. "Yeah! Oh Mommy, can we? Please?"

"But you gotta get into the bath so I can get you cleaned up before everybody gets here."

I imagine actually sitting at the dinner table with Scooby-Doo and Shaggy. I have no choice. "Okay!" I sprint for the stairs.

"Wait! Let's make sure they all can make it first."

My mother goes to the rotary phone on the wall. I stand by her side, growing ever more pleasantly agitated as she places the necessary phone calls. "Hi, Shaggy? This is Deborah, Aaron's mom? Oh, he's great. We were just wondering if you'd like to come over for dinner tonight? Oh great! So we'll see you later then. Okay, bye." And so on until the whole Scooby gang is invited.

I scurry up the stairs as fast as I can in my slippery-footed pajamas.

After the bath she dresses me in a button shirt with a little blue clip-on bow tie. Even my mom gets dressed up for company, with her earrings and makeup on.

The table is set for seven. Scooby, Shaggy, Fred, Daphne and Velma have all promised their attendance.

"Oh! That must be them!." Mom exclaims as she puts the food down and the finishing touches on the table. I must have missed the knock at the door, but I run from the kitchen with my mother to answer it. She stands in the open doorway greeting each guest coming through the door.

"Hi, Daphne!" A hug and a kiss for Fred. A pat on the head for Scooby, who arrives last (I was secretly nervous that he would cancel at the last minute). Then we all sit down. Mom serves me and herself and then doles out what I can only assume is my father's portion of the meal onto five clean dishes.

My mother and I eat our dinner together, empty chairs around a table of full plates. She asks Daphne how she keeps her hair so pretty while tracking clues through all those swamps and haunted houses. We all crack up laughing when Shaggy opens his mouth to reveal his chewed-up mashed potatoes.

~

Had the neighbors seen my mother hugging invisible people at the front door? Or the two of us at a fully set table, food on every plate, surrounded by empty seats? Mom didn't seem to care. When dinner was over she stood in the doorway waving goodbye to no one. Then she put me to bed. Dad still wasn't home, but I didn't notice.

Dale Mackey

Elegy for Summer

Down here
when you say
"put it up,"
it means
what we mean
when we say
"put it away"
up North.
At summer's start
we put up the net,
by which I mean
we stood it up,
staked it in,
batted birdies
and insults
over its head.
Now it's colder.
We've put it up,
by which I mean
we took it down,
balled up the net,
left a knot
we'll untangle
when we
put it up again.

Brian Griffin

Sunset at the Field Pond

It was not death, for I stood up
And all the dead lie down – Emily Dickinson

Not simple death or hidden night,
not spreading evening frost or fire–
it's just a splash of scalding light,
perfect chaos, shredded air.

If this new frame to fit my life
can cup a pond of cloud and sky,
the water-strider's rippling knife
can slice the mirror from my eye,

can bathe it all, elastic tears
that stretch and ooze reflected cloud,
amoebic, reaching for the years
that fled with those who now lie dead.

Sun's eye spills light, drips rust
on ripple, tree and spit-strewn sand.
The pond spreads pink: stained cloud, cold dusk
outside the night, the hard dark hand.

Judy S. Blackstock
    "Diversity at Its Best"

Janie Dempsey Watts

Moon Ride, Summer 1959

Moonlight spilled through the split in the gingham curtains. Earlier it had been almost, but not quite, hot enough for the cicadas to cease their nightly serenade, but after midnight, the heat had given way to a nighttime freshness. A light breeze rippled through the leaves of the crabapple tree just outside the window of the still sleeping girl who lay inside, dreaming of riding her horse.

They were running through the tall fescue, the girl's legs wrapped around the mare's wide body, her rhythm linked to the mare's. In the girl's mind, this forward, rolling motion was a circle, or Ferris wheel, of sorts. As they galloped forward, the girl's head rose up to the top of the invisible wheel, then to the front and back down again. She never tired of it, this forward, circular pattern that accompanied the horse's canter. Alone on her Ferris wheel, the wind blowing against her face, she was high up, safe from the world.

~

It was a soft blowing noise that finally tempted young Iris off the Ferris wheel of her dreams and the soft, cotton-sheeted bed, over to the open window where Powder beckoned, her white body outlined by silvery light. The girl quietly pushed against the window screen and eased out onto the mare's wide back. Even though it wasn't a cool night, Iris was dressed in a paper-thin nightgown and the heat of her horse felt good against her bare legs. She guided the horse under the crabapple tree, past her dad's new red '59 Chevy truck, to the edge of the fenced yard. There, she leaned down low over Powder's neck, unlatched the gate, and headed down the lane.

Not much moonlight reached the windows of Marvelous' cabin, where she lived with her father. The cabin was built in a low place where no one else wanted to build: too near to the stream, some thought, and certainly within the 100-year flood line. Some folks made fun of the cabin, but Marvelous and her daddy thought it was perfect. They got to stay there for free, as long as her daddy worked for the widow woman, Iris' grandmother. Surrounded by trees and cooled by the stream, the cabin, in its low place, was sheltered from the harsher weather and the prying eyes of neighbors. On hot nights like this one, living near running water in a thick stand of trees, in the lowest dip of the Valley, had its advantages. *Any plain fool knows heat rises, so we'll have the last laugh,* her daddy had often said. While the rest of the town sweltered, they were comfortable. Her father's snoring, coming loudly but comfortingly from the next room, was proof enough, if anyone needed it. Lying asleep in her cool sheets, Marvelous was awakened by a light tapping sound.

She jumped up and ran over to the window, pulled back the old flour sack curtains and saw the pale, grinning face of her best friend, Iris, motioning her to come outside. Marvelous sneaked through the living room where her father slept, carefully timing her steps to his breathing-in snores, so loud they would drown out the noise of the creaking floor. She didn't know what Iris wanted, but she was probably up to some mischief; that's why she liked her. Once Marvelous was outside, Iris offered a hand and pulled her up onto the mare. They would ride double, Iris in front.

"Hang on," Iris instructed, "and don't you let go." Marvelous did as she was told. At eight, Iris was a whole year older and knew her way with horses. Soon they were off, riding in the moonlight, two girls in nightgowns, one white, one black, their giggles trailing behind.

~

The harsh glare of the moonlight agitated Gandy as he tossed around in his gritty bed. Working in the fields had its price, he had said more than once. He never seemed to get the dirt off his boots, and the boots tracked it into the house, and even if he swept it, which wasn't that often, he couldn't seem to get all the grainy stuff off the floors, and certainly not off his feet or out of his bed. He kicked away the scratchy sheets that had irritated his burning skin all night. Working in the hot sun had its price. He hated these full moons that kept him awake through the long, scorching nights. His house was small and stuffy and not sufficient for a man who worked as hard as he did, he told himself. He needed his sleep. In another few hours he'd be back on the tractor, making a swath with the mower through the tall grass at the farm a few miles up the road. Haying season meant 14-hour days.

The white light persisted in torturing him through the cracks around the faded curtains. He swung his big feet off the bed, pulled on some old coveralls that were slightly stiff from the sweat of the day before, put his bare feet into the boots and headed for the back door of his sweltering, small brick house, as hot as the inside of a barbeque pit.

~

Riding as one on Powder, the two girls moved through Grandma's field. They were a paddleboat, cutting a wake behind them in the silver-green grass. The wind blew in their hair as they cantered along, moving together in an up-and-down rolling movement. It was Marvelous who first began to hum the tune, then to sing the words.

Bringing in the sheaves, bringing in the sheaves," her thin, high voice accompanied the thudding of the horse's hooves. Iris joined her.

"Bringing in the sheaves, we shall come rejoicing, bringing in the sheaves," they sang together as the mare's hooves rose up through the sea of grass, creating a wide circle through the field.

~

Sometimes walking helped Gandy sleep. He unclipped his German shepherds from the rope and signaled them to follow as he set out at a fast pace towards the ridge crest. He stood at the top, surveying the sweep of high grass he'd cut for the last two summers but would not be mowing tomorrow. No, Widow Woman Tucker had seen fit to hire someone else to take his place, a colored man.

As he looked out over the field he would probably never mow again, he reached down, grasped a bunch of tall blades with his stubby, tobacco-stained fingers and yanked up, ripping the plant from the ground, roots and all. He looked up and saw something cutting through the grass and felt a shiver pass over his bare arms as he heard the voices singing, *"We shall come rejoicing."* A white horse was gliding along through the too-tall grass not fifty feet away. Two small riders rode the horse, the one in front pale as the moon and the one behind dark as cocoa. He collected his dogs.

"Sic 'em, boys!" he commanded. The shepherds bolted off toward their prey.

~

The girls were laughing their way through the second chorus of "Bringing in the Sheaves" when it happened. Sensing danger, the horse spooked and turned abruptly, causing the riders to spin forward like an out-of-control Ferris wheel come loose from its moorings. The twosome tumbled forward and landed all at once in the soft grass, knocking the breath out of both. Powder recovered and, frightened, bolted away.

On the ground, Marvelous still clung to Iris, as she'd been instructed, her arms wrapped tightly around her friend's waist, even though they were lying on their sides on the cool grass. As soon as Iris caught her breath, she spoke.

"You can let go now," she said. Marvelous loosened her hands and sat up and saw nothing but the surrounding wall of grass.

"Where's Powder?" she asked. But before Iris could answer, they heard a nearby rustle and a low growling noise. They reached out for one another, grasped hands and stood up to confront danger together.

The heads of two ugly dogs appeared through the tall grass, less than four feet away. Iris knew those dogs, how mean they were—almost, Grandma had said, mean as their owner, Mr. Gandy, whom she'd had to let go. One of them lunged forward, snarling. There was no point in running—they had outrun and killed a terrier last year.

"Go away!" Iris yelled, and flung her fist out in a hitting motion. But the largest dog only briefly recoiled, then moved in closer, lowering its head.

Iris pushed Marvelous behind her, shielded her, preparing for the worst. Her heart beat hard and strong, and at first Marvelous thought the drumming noise was coming from Iris' chest.

Iris felt the vibration through the ground and realized the pounding of hooves signaled the arrival of Powder. The curs heard it too and looked around, but saw nothing until the sharp hooves crashed through the tall grass and landed directly on their big heads. The shepherds yelped and cowered and ran away as quickly as they'd appeared.

"Scaredy cats," Iris said. Both girls began to shake and laugh with relief. Powder nodded her head up and down and offered her silky muzzle. Iris stroked the mare and thanked her while Marvelous simply flung her thin arms around the horse's damp chest. After a few minutes had passed, Iris hoisted herself up on the mare's back, pulled Marvelous up behind her and set off.

~

Some distance away, Gandy bent down to examine his dogs in the moonlight but there appeared to be no permanent damage and that was a good thing. He would have made Widow Tucker pay for it. He shivered as he stared across the field, over the tall grass he should be rightly mowing tomorrow but wasn't. All on account of the coloreds, one of them singing at this moment as pretty as she pleased, and with a white girl. What was the world coming to?

~

Iris got Marvelous back home well before the roosters began to stir. By the time Iris made it home to her own bed, the cicadas had ceased their night song. A gentle wash of moonlight spilled through her curtains. She closed her eyes and tried not to think of the dogs. Instead she imagined galloping again through the field atop Powder, her friend Marvelous tucked behind her. They would move in a forward motion, like a Ferris wheel, high up on a horse, together safe from the world.

Michael Gill

Strange Pigtails

I was riding in the car with my Daddy on his day off – I think we had gone to the old Sears and Roebuck – back in the day before shopping malls, when Sears was called Sears and Roebuck, and there was just one in Knoxville, in their own building on top of the hill at Central Street & Baxter Avenue. Must have been around 1960.

Anyway, we were headed home, in no particular hurry. Daddy liked to drive around different places just to see what he could see, and I noticed that we were in a part of town where the Negroes lived. There were kids about my age playing outside, along the street. The girls all had pigtails, but they were strange pigtails, not like the ones I was used to. Instead of two pigtails symmetrically situated on the left and right of the back of their heads like all the ones I had ever seen, there were four and five and six and maybe even seven or eight pigtails scattered over the backs and sides and tops and even the fronts of their heads! What was this? Didn't they know how to do it? Didn't their mamas know?

And then the thought came to me. It was a revelation! They – these girls and their mamas – surely knew about the usual pigtails that the little white girls wore, and they surely could make them that way if they wanted, but they didn't. They liked them other ways, all kinds of ways! And it was okay.

In fact, it was wonderful. I was too young to understand it then, but those strange pigtails had created a crack in the walls of conformity that might otherwise have imprisoned me, and I could see through that crack a world that was much bigger and more marvelous than I had ever before dreamed.

Jan Perkins

Jedediah

Those who sought change always left the tiny Tennessee town where I grew up. It's pretty much the same as it was the summer Saturday morning my cousin Jed and I inspected the new sewage system the mayor decided we needed and his brother built. We traced the effluent until it disappeared down a hole. Then we had to know where it went.

"Papaw's got some dye left over from his dry-cleaning and dyeing business nobody's ever gonna miss," Jed said. We sneaked through the woods that shroud stills closed until corn harvest, when the corn would be mashed and strained for dead roaches and mice before sale to tourists who hear "It's good fer what ails ye" and "Us hillbillies lives on it." We dump gallon after gallon of concentrated red dye down the disappearing hole.

We go home silenced by that code of honor that lets thieves live lawless lives. We awaken Sunday morning to shrieks. "The water's bloody!" "The Lord's sent a plague! "The end of time's a-comin!"

"This ain't no good situation," Jed whispered.

"You mean, because we flush the john and it's right back in the sink?"

"No, because when people get real scared and then find out somebody's just played a trick on 'em, they're awful mad at 'em."

"Uh-huh. And being kids won't be no protection?"

We decided to hoot, howl and holler just like everybody else but without overdoing it, since saying "no" too loud is saying "yes."

We were hurried along to church that morning to hear Preacher Moneymaker pray for the plague to be lifted. He promised that all who were saved and came to church and tithed would not need to worry. "If the end of time's comin', the Good Lord will rapture us before things get bad. Maybe He's just warnin' us about lettin' outsiders come in and contaminate our community."

Jed and I prayed silently that no one ever found us out. They never did and the water cleared two days later.

Deacon Jedediah is now a pillar of the community in the same Tennessee mountain town, raising his children in the same church.

Marilyn Kallet

Dog Days

Gigi, my mother's miniature,
barked at Volkswagens.
"And she hated the smell
of coloreds!" Mother bragged.
No black people

came to our door
on Coleridge Road. None
permeated the perimeter.
Mom had planted a black jockey
on our front lawn.

One block away, whites only
caddied at the Club.
We Jews weren't

in the swim.
You would have had to be dead

not to smell the fear
that soaked my working-class childhood
like a sprinkler in the fifties,
our soggy upper-middle crust
in the sixties,

and after. Was it fear
that turned our collie
mean? Mama had Lady
"put to sleep."
And if she was kinder

to the cute poodle than to the rest
of us, who could blame her?
When I was four, Mama
permed me
to look like her toy.

My scalp scalded, hair fried.
Scared straight since.
Dogs were better at obeying
than we were, better
at unconditional love.

Lady aimed to kill everything
that moved.
Spared Mother's hands, though.
Licked her Alpo-scented fingers,
bathed and bathed those tough red nails.

Dick Penner

"Martin Luther King Day, January 2000"

Peggy Douglas

Operation Dixie

> *Don't strike back or curse if abused . . .*
> *show yourself courteous at all times . . .*
> *remember love and nonviolence.*
> – SNCC Code of Conduct (1960)

I'm looking at a photo of me and Johnnie
sitting in a booth of the Woolworth's
luncheonette in downtown Chattanooga
snapped a few minutes before seven boys
dared to be served. I saw their dark
silhouettes in button-down shirts
and dress trousers sitting on red vinyl
stools under the Whites Only sign.

I heard the rabble of slack-jawed,
Confederate-flag-waving, fit-to-kill
white boys gathered like dogs–
not the kind who wag their tails
while growling so it's hard to tell
which end to believe. These barks
were painfully clear: *Hey, you can't*
buy a malted milk with a welfare check.
Try hanging it over the Tennessee River
to see if it'll get your cousin to surface.

Today's Special swung from gold
chains over the lunch counter:
Liver and onions, $2.99. Underneath,
a fountain girl with a no-nonsense air
sliced lettuce and tomatoes to avoid

steadfast eyes peering through racks
of mops and brooms at the back counter.
A triple-dip banana split was thirty-nine
cents, strawberry shortcake pennies less
and I wondered who would pay the price.

Willa Schneberg

I

> *Chang Bunker (May 11, 1811-January 17, 1874) and Eng Bunker
> May 11, 1811-January 17, 1874) were the original "Siamese
> Twins."*

Not until after I felt the moist soil
of our Mount Airy farm
between the fingers on the hand
that reaches out to the world,
the one free of my brother,
did I understand that Chang,
who stinks of rum,
is not me.

When it is time to reside
at the other house,
Chang's wife's home,
I go in body only and recite to myself
My dear Thomas Hardy:

Jewels in joy designed
To ravish the sensuous mind
Lie lightless, all their sparkles bleared and black and blind.

While Adelaide, more active than women
With singletons need to be, rides Chang,
I daydream of our cows, their udders turgid
Until farmhands relieve them and milk
Squirts into tin pails, and I wonder about

The young beggar without hands or feet
To whom I gave twenty dollars
Towards his own bit of land.

Here, dead leaves birth humus
and on my back porch
raindrops pool in privacy.

Grace would be to sit by myself
in a room with the door closed
upon a chair built for one.

J.L. Hensley

Mexican Minute

Lines composed upon a barstool
At Jose's Corsair Cantina
Ziahuatanejo, Guerro, Mexico
January, 2005

Jose leans on his bar near the *propina* jar
Watching the gringos go by.
He flashes a grin and says, "*Senors!* Come in!"
Then they're caught by the gleam in his eye.

He says, "*Amigos*, a Cerveza Sol
With some lime and some salt on the glass
Will help you forget all the problems you left
And in a minute your troubles are past."

Chorus:
Just a Mexican minute, and you will be in it
That heaven that's old Mexico.
No hurry, no worry, no ice, no snow flurry
Happiness? Zihuatanejo!

There was a smile on his face when we left that place,
And dropped some pesos into his jar.
He said, "*Amigos*, you've earned the lesson you've learned:
That you've got to slow down to go far!"

Chorus:
Just a Mexican minute, and you will be in it
That heaven that's old Mexico.
No hurry, no worry, no ice, no snow flurry
Happiness? Zihuatanejo!

Now we're back in the States, same old rats in the race,
And the clocks are all running on time.
But I sure miss Jose and the Mexican way
Of mixing life with some salt and some lime.

Chorus:
Just a Mexican minute, and you will be in it
That heaven that's old Mexico.
No hurry, no worry, no ice, no snow flurry
Happiness? Zihuatanejo!

propina = tip

Connie Jordan Green

Pastoral

My dad and the bull stand side by side,
pasture fence stretched tight, garage
in the background where my grandfather
parked his Ford truck, staircase rising
to attic storage, dust motes in afternoon
sun, pungent smell of oily rags, crankcase
fluids. My dad is sixteen or seventeen,
slight body beginning to muscle out
to the shape he'll carry into adulthood.
In the photo, the bull is docile,
as all animals were around my dad, could
be the family dog waiting to have his ears
scratched. This is the bull of family stories,
raised on a bottle, groomed and petted,
recipient of blue ribbons at county fairs,
my dad the only one who could step
into a pasture with him, money from his sale
sending Daddy to Virginia Polytechnic Institute
for a dreamed-of year before banks failed,
the country shut down; he went off
to the mining camps, a second chapter written
with marriage, family, labor so different
from the first. His daughters gaze in wonder
at the picture, only his crooked smile to say
this was once my life.

D. Antwan Stewart

Ennui

~ *Knoxville, Tennessee*

A secretary riding the late-night Magnolia sings her
40-Acres-and-a-Mule song.
Some nights she drowses or dozes off to sleep completely,
the bus rattling down Gay Street to Summit Hill
and Broadway, turning toward her neighborhood
of potholes and teenagers playing chicken
in the middle of the road. Some nights she sings the latest blows
she's been dealt: minimum-wage paychecks too small to buy
a new alternator for the car; rent increase on the duplex and no money
to hire anyone to re-caulk the bathroom, re-support the sagging roof,
return the baby possum in the kitchen to its mother.
Her food stamp card reads a low balance, barely any food left
in the cabinets and what's in the freezer is freezer-burnt,
though she'll eat it — she has no choice.
She'll dust the ice crystals off the way she dusts off anything
and will eat with a solemn determination,
feed the children & bathe them,
whisk them off to bed without a story because she's worked all day
constructing a living she'll die before ever quitting. So she rides the bus
to save for Christmases and birthdays and the Fourth of July,
so her children will know at least minor joy. She rises in the morning
to pour cereal or oatmeal for the briefest breakfast
around the family table
because that's what her children want.
It's better than being sent off early to school
for a meal someone else pays for;
someone else who's afforded the luxury

of real butter, bacon perfectly crisp, syrup glistening brown in sunlight
filtering through the white-washed kitchen, floors of marble stone and
stainless steel appliances wedged between cherry oak cupboards
and Lazy Susans. Who'd begrudge a secretary who wants a home
filled with vases of perennials fragrant
with bright blossoms and staunch stems,
not to mention dishwashing machines that don't even whisper?
and what a godsend to own liquor cabinets of single malts
and temperature-controlled *cruvinets?* By the smile on her face
could this be what she dreams about on a crowded bus,
holding onto the rail because no one believes in affection
for the weary on the Magnolia? With any hope, she won't
arrive home needing to iron the children's school clothes
or scrub the bathtub
or call animal control to catch a possum she finds has returned
trapped in the corner behind the stove. She'd rather sip cheap vodka
with pomegranate juice—as it makes the sin go down more easily,
and is delicious, makes her
forget she has to work a double the next day
with no time between shifts
to grab a five-dollar footlong at Subway or catch an episode
of *The Young & the Restless.*
No wonder her head nods with the constant beat
of *tick-tock tick-tock tick-tock.*
She prays to have the energy of several people living inside her body,
to have ample time to lean on her mop for a reprieve
from domestic work, or on a break from the typing pool, dream
of a life where it's possible to buy a more opulent toilet
each time someone takes a shit that stains the porcelain,
as this means she'll no longer have to ride the bus
and never have to witness
another woman standing in the exit to take a piss or endure a man

with Tourette's sitting next to her because he insists on it,
because he doesn't understand
how this disturbs her from the first chance she's had to sleep all day.

Eli Mitchell

Blood's Thicker

"Poor Reathel," he says, shaking his pinched head, "she didn't have
no prayer. She was sunk from the get-go."

A scruffy teenager, his gaunt jaws are chewing Red Man. Eyes at
half-mast.

"Now, Mama and me never did pay her no mind. But, to tell you the
honest-to-God truth, she was a good'un. That Reathel treated me right
kindly, just like I was a little puppy or somethin'." His voice cracked,
"And we was only married going on a year or so."

He and I are slopping about in mud near the cockeyed door of his
double-wide. Through the torn screen, I get a broadside of Big Mama, a
large, bath-robed figure fussing over a grimy stove, splattered with
grease. Her thick arms look better suited for lifting the refrigerator than
for flipping Spam. Trash litters the linoleum. Red Dog beer cans crowd
the table and accent Elvis' black-velvet portrait tacked to the wall. A
towheaded Jesus hangs over a La-Z-Boy chair.

Glaring at a rumpled pile of clothes on something resembling a
couch, Big Mama growls, "Reathel couldn't have kept a decent house if
her life. . . . *And* she sure ain't—weren't—blood either."

The kid kicks a bent beer can aside and talks at his muddy boots.
"Started drinking again, can't seem to hep it." Sigh. "So somehow them
Red Cross people down there in Knoxville heared about the drownin'?
And sent y'uns up here?"

I answer yes; I'm a Red Cross volunteer, here to see if we can help
with the funeral expenses.

"Yeah," he chuckles, pointing a bony finger at me, "And you're in the *Volunteer* State, ain't ya. Ha!"

Then he says soberly, "Care to take a gander at my car?" Brown spittle shoots through his pursed lips, splashes in muck. Toward the screen door he whines, "Mama, you wouldn't be ill if we was to go over and take a look at that mess, now would you?"

Big Mama lists our way, reaches out her ham hock arm and slams the aluminum door: *bam!* It rebounds back at her and she bellows, "Jesus *Christ!*"

The kid whispers, "Well, mama's been het up ever since Reathel and me eloped. She gets worser every day. I don't dare to even *mention* Reathel's name at all."

I follow him, slogging through a car graveyard, minor league for East Tennessee. No more than a dozen rusting hulks. Three geriatric Ford pickups. A flat-tired, two-tone '55 Chevy, dirty white, baby blue. Beyond a Fury, reared up on two blocks, sits the carapace of a VW Bug. A dogwood has grown up through its shattered front windshield.

He catches me staring at the Bug and mutters, "Them Jap cars never was good for nuttin', anyways."

Past the dogwood, about to bloom, we work our way around tree stumps and mud-splattered whitewalls. From the tasseling maples on the ridge, a wood hen cackles. An April breeze lifts a Monarch over our heads. A late sun edges inside a neglected shed and glints off something chrome.

"See that weird-looking machine in there? That air is what they call an epileptic exercise trainer thang. Mama just got me that yesterday." He spoke as if she did him proud. "It's for me to become more aerobatic, you know, so as I don't bust a gut or somethin'. She don't want me lifting them barbells no more like them movie stars do, you know, like Sylvester Swarts-a-majigger and that bunch does. 'Blessed are the meek,' she says. 'Blessed are the meek.' I reckon she's right on."

We splash through a mud puddle to get to a yellow Camaro. The windows are down and vent mildew. A reeking thing.

"Say," he asks, "does the Red Cross help a body fix his car back up?"

"No, I'm sorry, we can't do anything like that," I reply. "Tell me, what happened?"

"Well, we was heading for the Monster Mash—you know, down at the arena where they have them Big Wheel vehicles, and they crush cars under 'em? And there's tractor pulls and stuff? Well, we was going down there and it's apouring down the rain. Cats, dogs . . . frogs. Had been for days."

He stops, gets a chew out of his back pocket and offers me some. I say, "No thanks . . . . Who all was with you?"

"Mama. And my wife, Reathel. Uh, she was my wife. Anyway, Reathel didn't much want to go. To tell you the truth, she was madder than a hornet. She never did take to big events like that. She'd much rather dress up, fit to kill, and go dancing at the AMVETS or somethin'. 'For Godsake, leave your mama at home,' she'd always say. Now, Mama . . . Mama loves to be taken to them Mashes better'n a hog loves to wallow."

He peers into the soggy front seat and says, "Mama always sits shotgun. She claims to get car pukin' if she's in the back." With his thumb he points to the Camaro's cramped rear seat. "And Reathel was right cheer.

"Like I say, it come down in buckets and once we passed the Old Fort hysterical marker and got on down to the creek—that's Frog Level Creek I'm talking about—when we got there it was plumb over the road. Reathel hollered 'Lord, don't drive into that!' But, like I say, we never did pay her no mind. Man, I wish I'd have jerked up and took notice that time. Mama and me didn't reckon it was *that* deep, so we crept on out there . . . right into that stinkin' river.

"Boy!" he shouts as he slaps the top of the car, "it musta been up to our necks. I had no ideal how deep it was, and none of us could swim a lick. That was about when Reathel started screaming bloody murder. All of the sudden we was movin' and floatin' and driftin' and we swang crosswise to the road . . . and then we was pointin' upstream. I was hepless. I couldn't get aholt of the reins. This here thing," he reaches through the window and grabs a knob fastened to the steering wheel, "this here nigger-knob just spun around crazylike."

His mucid spit lands hard on the tire. "Mama yelled, 'Sonny, roll down the goddamn window' . . . but I shouldn't have done that. That crick just poured in. You could've caught a trout outta that back seat. So I clum out of the window onto the roof. And I clung on by my fingernails. So-hep-me-God, I did. Then I was areachin' for Reathel way in the back . . . ."

He pauses, looks toward the trailer, then whispers, "But Mama latched onto my arm like a pit bull and wouldn't turn loose. Her being my mama and all, I just *had* to get her out of thatair window first."

Staring into the sodden back seat, he whines, "After that, poor Reathel, she didn't even have a bitty prayer. My mamma was petrified—bless her heart—had me in one of them vise-grip chokeholds. I tried to get in there again—to pull Reathel outta there, but all I could do was to get a glimpse. She was way underwater. Her eyes was real wide andher mouth . . . her mouth was slack like she was going to yawn forever or somethin'."

~

"Sonny!"

Her bark startles us. His mother is standing by the shed, hands on hips, glaring at me. "Tell that man you ain't got no more time to answer his stupid questions," she yells. "Besides, your supper's gettin' cold."

Big Mama wheels around and storms toward the trailer. He seems dragged in her direction like a kite on a string, bouncing across the ground. I take several large strides to catch up with him.

"So, to finish this whole thing off, somehow Mama and me worshed up okay. Last I seen of Reathel . . . she was just abobblin' downstream in my car. It sorta looked like a great big yellow runaway fishing cork. I just couldn't have gotten her outta there. No way in Hell. Like I say, Reathel didn't have no prayer."

As we near the double-wide, I think I see his eyes get watery.

Chin down on his concave chest, he whispers, "It's a good thing Jesus is the forgivin' sort, ain't it?"

Willa Schneberg

Tiny Monuments

For David Maisel, who photographed canisters holding the ashes of mental patients at a state hospital in Oregon.

When human beings were still locked away
for sadness clinging to them like a marine layer,
hearing voices telling them how awful they were,
going fetal when cars backfired or corks popped,
they were housed at the Oregon State Insane Asylum,
and when they ceased to be, they were cremated.

If no one claimed a brother, a daughter, or a father,
the ashes were kept in numbered copper canisters,
on pine shelves in an underground vault.
Not infrequently the water table rose up
on its tiptoes to flick its wand coated
with efflorescence and mineral dazzle,
 to give the forgotten inside corroded containers
homes uniquely their own, where an alchemy
of copper and water bloomed
on their surfaces and burst into color.

These tiny monuments to the scorned and unknown
wear patinas of pink, burnt sienna, ocher, aqua,
and if you look closely you can find
moon craters, archipelagos, frozen waterfalls,
dunes with lone tracks, and Big Dippers
embedded in their pores.

Artress Bethany White

Bone and Socket

for Bennie White

She made eating chicken bones
look like a fine art.
Picture this:
a plate of wings deep-fried
to perfection
and an ice cold beer,
so chilly you had to wrap a
paper towel around it to handle.

As the conversation heated up,
those bones started snapping.
The soft, spongy bone tips nibbled
and chewed before the marrow
was sucked out like a milkshake through a straw.
The watching was more educational
than Mr. Sullivan's
high school anatomy and physiology
where everyone earned an A,
a consequence of his weak bladder
and our unwillingness to pass up
an opportunity to cheat.

This study of bones
had to be a byproduct of the Depression era
I reasoned
when people learned not to waste anything
like the marrow,
a second meal after the meat was gone.

I can still feel the pinch of my cousin's
grip on my arm as I went to throw
the smallest bone
of the chicken wing in the trash,
that grip that stopped me
mid-toss as she said
Uh-uh, girl, give it here,
that's the best part.

Linda Parsons Marion

Sukiyaki

My stepmother stirred swift tides of soy and sesame, strange sea
bubbling dark. Nights she rocked that samurai blade, flank or
roundsteak soaking the drainboard, a brace of greentailed scallions
hacked headless. Taught the ancient ways by her brother's war bride,
who shadowed him to Tennessee with eyes downcast, she sugared the
beef, dipped in beaten egg bright as rising suns. I entered her kitchen
like a bamboo grove, part paradise, part unknowable, exotic as distant
Osaka. Raised on Boyardee and La Choy,

I stepped from one slippery shore to another, from
my mother's cold shoulder to steam rising on ribboned
onions, red meat cut on the bias. Ricebowl filled,
I ladled an extra sorghum-slow syllable, *suk-i-ya-ki,*
my tongue trying new salt.

Richard P. Remine
"Dolly Parton Look-Alikes"

174

John C. Mannone

Taste East Tennessee

Dis-moi ce que tu manges, je te dirai ce que tu es.
Tell me what you eat and I will tell you what you are. — Anthelme
Brillat-Savarin

We are sugar-sweet iced tea, Southern hospitality,
fried chicken, turnip greens with a touch of vinegar;
pinto beans, yellow cornbread and chow-chow.
We are better than any whip-creamed banana pudding,
without the whiskey. Fried apple pie and JFG coffee.
Pecan pie, too. Sourwood honey on homemade bread.
Or some Cocke County kudzu jelly on wheat toast.
A bit of ramps with poke salad and deep-fried pork rinds.
We are Moon Pies and RC Colas, a little Rocky Top
with that Mountain Dew. And some hickory-smoked
pork barbeque, baked beans, deviled eggs and coleslaw.
Grainger County tomatoes—fried green. County fair
corndogs and funnel cakes. Anyway-you-cook-it corn
on the cob slathered with butter. Salt and pepper, please.
We are Bro' Jack's wet rub on ribs, and hushed-up catfish.
Mustard greens and any type of food with soul:
Black-eyed peas and collard greens. Mac and cheese,
especially for the potluck supper after Sunday church.
We are cathead biscuits and sawmill gravy, country
ham and grits. Wampler's farm sausage. Red-eye gravy.
Fountain City burgers, and my auntie's applesauce
stack cakes. Crockpot venison, and just plain old deer
jerky. We are thank-you-Lord-for-this-food Southern
Baptist and just about any other denomination, or non.
Pass the Krispy Kreme donuts, please. And amen to that.

Hector Qirko

Diversity

My father was Posidhon Qirko, and his was in many ways a classic American success story. He was born in 1922 in Nartë, Albania, a small, ethnically Greek community across the Adriatic from Italy's "boot heel." His father, Giovanni (nicknamed "Nako," my middle name), was a merchant in the town. He was a stern man who gave his children little praise. My father recalled that when he scored a goal for his school soccer team, his father didn't so much as look up from the stands—but did finally nod to him when he scored a second. Nako was imprisoned during World War II for refusing to cooperate with both the occupying Germans and the Albanian Communists who ran them out of the country. I don't know much about my father's mother, Olga, except that she was tall and fair—like many Albanians, of northern European ancestry. She died when he was very young.

Long before the war, Nako decided that my father would be the son to succeed him in running the business, and so invested in his education. He sent Posidhon first to boarding school in Corfu, Greece, and later to the University of Padua in Italy, where he was enrolled when the conflict of WW II began. My father didn't talk much about those years, although he did tell me that like many of his fellow students, he had taken to the hills and waited out Mussolini's Fascists and, later, the German troops. The students engaged in relatively minor acts of resistance—tearing down handbills, lighting fires, and the like.

When the war ended, the Communists ran Albania, Nako was in prison, and Posidhon was advised that it was not safe to return home. Although he faithfully sent money to his family throughout his life, it would be forty-five years before his first visit back. I'm not sure what he did to survive in those lean post-war years, but he told me that he sometimes picked up a little cash gambling on chess and bridge. (He was extremely good at both.) In 1948 he was given the opportunity, as a "Displaced Person," to emigrate to England, Australia, or the United States, if he could find a sponsor. As he had an aunt in New York City who guaranteed him a job as a busboy, he came to the U.S. He already spoke four languages. While signing up to take English classes he met my mother, Clara Corina Delgado, a Cuban, and so began to learn two more. He and my mother married and, once each reached the required years of residency, became American citizens.

After holding down a number of low-paying jobs, he got a break. A friend of one of my mother's brothers arranged an interview for him at a large chemical and pharmaceutical company, American Cyanamid, whose consumer divisions made Formica, Old Spice, Breck shampoo, and Pine-Sol. His soon-to-be boss, Rudy Ephrussi, saw something in Posidhon and offered him a position as an assistant clerk. The job, however, paid less than the one he had at the time, as an elevator operator. My father often said that my mother had to persuade him to take it. He was thirty-two, had a new son (me), and still had barely adequate English skills.

Once he settled into the job, he saw the opportunities it presented, especially when his boss suggested that he enroll in night classes in accounting at Pace College in Lower Manhattan. A year or two later the company needed to send someone to Italy to help the head of a recently purchased subsidiary with his books. When his boss stepped in and recommended my father, off he went, for a full year. The rest of the family (now including my sister Ingrid Olga), spent the duration in Cuba. The stay in Italy launched his career, and my father never forgot what Ephrussi did for him. For many years, he visited him every time he went to American Cyanamid's home office. My mother recalls the day Posidhon got word of his old boss's death over the phone. He wept openly—the only time she ever saw him do so.

My dad's talent for business, as well as his and my mother's willingness to live overseas, took him next to Caracas, Venezuela, to work as an assistant comptroller. That's where my second sister, Astrid Yvonne, was born. After that, we lived in Peru, Brazil (where he learned yet another language, Portuguese), Colombia, Venezuela again, and Mexico. We would stay two or three years in each country, as Posidhon made his way up the management ladder. He worked extremely hard, consistently delivered results, and was in all respects loyal to the company, so he was sent to the most problematic subsidiaries to turn them around. He also worked for several years in the company's headquarters in New Jersey, overseeing the Asian region, before taking his last troubleshooting assignment in Brazil. He retired there, as both president of the large subsidiary and a vice-president of the parent corporation. After retirement he worked as a consultant with various companies until his death. As I said: a classic Amercian success story.

However, my father viewed his career a little differently than do those who know only what is sketched above. He was grateful for his opportunities and proud of his successes, but also frustrated. At many steps along the way, he saw others who he said were less qualified move up the ranks faster than he did, and sometimes he found himself working for people he had trained. The path to the highest management levels required a position in the company's U.S. headquarters, but his opportunity for such a position was repeatedly delayed because, his superiors argued, he was too valuable in the field to bring home. By the time he was positioned for a shot at the company's presidency, he was described as too old, and the top job went instead to another of those who had trained and worked under him.

I can't know how accurate his view of his career trajectory was, but I do know that my father always felt that his background kept him from progressing past a certain point. He hadn't attended the same colleges as the other top executives. He hadn't spent much time in the United States. He never lost his foreign accent, humor, or style, and he thought these made his bosses in the home office uncomfortable. He once told me that upon his arrival in New York, he had considered changing his name to Don Kirk (his nickname was "Dony"), and that perhaps he should have done so. While he never described it as overt, discrimination was part and parcel of his view of the American experience.

I've often thought of my father in my years in East Tennessee working in the field of organizational diversity. I think his story illustrates two key points regarding diversity management.

The first is that "white male" is a term which, like other terms denoting ethnic or demographic groups, hides so much variability as to be essentially useless. My father was a white male, true; but so were most of his employers and colleagues. He was nevertheless different from them to a degree that, at least in his mind, limited his opportunities.

The second point is that ultimately no one can judge whether another person is achieving his or her full potential. My father's career was a successful one by almost any standard. But if you'd asked him, he would have said that he was never given the chance to contribute to his fullest. Organizations use many measures to try to assess their effectiveness in promoting and achieving diversity. For instance, they might count the number of members of a particular group that reach management-level positions, and view increases over time as evidence that they're doing the right things. But one can never know how many of those individuals had the skills and ambition to achieve even more than they did. Full potential is an internal standard, one which external measures can never capture.

Roosevelt Thomas, in *Beyond Race and Gender,* wrote that managing diversity involves more than just opening the doors of schools, businesses, and other institutions to all people, because an open door does not guarantee full opportunity once inside. Nor is it sufficient to acknowledge, understand, or even celebrate differences, for the simple reason that you can't address, or even recognize, them all. There is no doubt that acknowledging historically underrepresented groups, especially those stigmatized by racial, ethnic, or gender bias, is an essential step in managing diversity. But every group so acknowledged, as well as many that are not, contains within it innumerable differences. Most people, like my father, don't fit neatly into categories–and trying to put them there perpetuates the very stigmatizing typologies that well-meaning organizations try to combat. To manage diversity truly and effectively, Thomas wrote, organizations must make the *structural* changes necessary to ensure that anyone, whatever his or her unique constellation of traits, has the opportunity to reach full potential.

So diversity is ultimately about organizations and their employees benefiting from an understanding of what is relevant to success and what is not. My father's unusual background as well as his managerial skills helped his company, but he believed that the former was underappreciated and, indeed, an obstacle to his progress. He might have tried to hide his uniqueness, as many have: change his name, conquer his accent, rewrite his life story, and bury his perspective. But then only his managerial skills would have been available to his company; it would have lost the full benefits that his background and experiences provided.

Effective diversity management, then, involves the use of *all* of the tools that an individual brings to the workplace—for the good of *both* the individual and the organization. I think that to my dad and any of us, that would be the true success story.

Valentino Constantinou

"Gay Street"

Contributors' Biographies

JENNIFER ALLDREDGE works for the Alliance to Save Energy, volunteers with Destination ImagiNation, is a member of SCBWI, and part of the Tennessee Stage Company, whose annual Shakespeare on the Square is the backdrop for this story. She moved to Knoxville from Franklin, Tennessee, five years ago. Jennifer is happily married to Greg and has two beautiful daughters, Kristen and Kt.

KB BALLENTINE received her MFA in Poetry from Lesley University, Cambridge, MA. Published in print and online journals, KB has two collections of poetry: *Fragments of Light* (2009) and *Gathering Stones* (2008), published by Celtic Cat, and is anthologized in *Southern Light: Twelve Contemporary Southern Poets*. A finalist for the 2006 Joy Harjo Award and 2007 finalist for the Ruth Stone Prize, KB also received Dorothy Sargent Rosenberg Memorial Funds in 2006 and 2007.

ROBERT L. BEASLEY is a retired Episcopal priest and sometime writer living in downtown Maryville, TN. Bob has published articles in *Honolulu* (with Martha Lee, his wife), *Your Church, The Witness, Group*, and a short story, "The Paved Road," in *The StoryTeller*. Bob is completing a novel tentatively entitled *Going Down With Bishop Robinson*.

JUDY S. BLACKSTOCK is a divorced mother of two, grandmother of three, sister, aunt, cousin and friend to a huge bevy of crazy people. Her interests include traveling, photography and writing. She holds special her family, pets, friends, Scrabble, Kenya, Sunset Beach, NC, and enjoying the beauty of East Tennessee. She declares she is interested in about anything except politics and humorless people. Appropriately, her motto is *Carpe diem!*

BARBARA BLOY "Though I admit to being a Yankee, my years at Maryville College and UT gave me plenty of time to fall for the many beauties of a place surrounded by highlands. I taught freshman writing at UT and played the guitar and sang ballads and other folk wonders at the immortal Mad Mouse on Cumberland Avenue."

JENNIFER HOLLIE BOWLES is the author of three poetry chapbooks and the editor of *The Medulla Review*

JEANNETTE BROWN writes poetry and fiction. Her work has been published in *Bellevue Literary Review, Southwestern American Literature, New Millennium Writings, Texas Observer, ArtSpace, Mother Earth, Breathing the Same Air — An East Tennessee Anthology, Suddenly IV, Knoxville Bound,* and other publications. She edited *Literary Lunch,* a Knoxville Writers' Guild food anthology.

JANET BROWNING received her degree in Art and Art Education from East Tennessee State University. After teaching art in public schools for seven years she founded ArtSmart Inc., an after-school art enrichment program. She also has worked as a portrait artist since the age of sixteen. She is now buying art from all over the world for resale in Hands Around the World, a shop on Main Street in Jonesborough, Tennessee.

ANDRE CANTY was born in 1985 and raised in East Knoxville. He graduated from South-Doyle High School in 2003 with awards in academics and athletics. He attended Middle Tennessee State University and earned a degree in English Literature from the University of Tennessee. He works as Assistant to the Director of the Beck Cultural Exchange Center and volunteers for many Knoxville nonprofits. He makes people laugh and think on Twitter and Facebook.

MARK DANIEL COMPTON founded the Southern Appalachian International Film Festival. Born and raised in South Carolina, he has accumulated a degree in Theology from Florida College, a Bachelor's degree in Theatre and Speech from the University of South Carolina, and a Master's degree from East Tennessee State University in Tourism Development. He plans to receive his MFA in Graphic Design & Time-Based Media from ETSU in December 2011. Mark has taught English, Media, and Cinema Studies for several colleges in East Tennessee.

VALENTINO CONSTANTINOU was born in Cyprus and has lived primarily in Knoxville since 1996. He currently lives in Melbourne, Australia, while he works towards his economics degree at the University of Tennessee. His first exhibition was in New York City's APW Gallery: the "Something Different" exhibition on July 17, 2009. His work has also been exhibited in Knoxville, Tennessee, at the Stir Fry Cafes, The Gallery, the Emporium, and the JulieApple Studio.

CLYDE CROSWELL was born in Memphis in 1945 and attended Memphis Central High School and the University of Tennessee in Knoxville. Dr. Croswell invested 29 years in the Marine Corps and achieved his Doctorate from George Washington University, where he teaches graduate studies. He is President of Community-L, Inc., an organizational development consulting firm, and he and his wife Mizue, a wood-firing ceramist, live at Eagle Peak in the northern Shenandoah Valley near Winchester, Virginia.

JUDY LOCKHART DiGREGORIO is retired from the U.S. Department of Energy, Oak Ridge Operations. She is a popular speaker and humor columnist whose work has appeared in anthologies and national magazines including *The Army Times*, *The Writer*, and the Chicken Soup books. Judy is the author of two humor books, *Life Among the Lilliputians* and *Memories of a Loose Woman*. Her CD of humorous stories is titled "Jest Judy." In her spare time Judy performs with a women's vocal group, Varying Degrees.

AARON DiMUNNO mostly writes nonfiction. He is currently between permanent residences, staying with friends when he can and chiseling away at a collection of short stories.

PEGGY DOUGLAS is a performance poet, musician, and college professor from Chattanooga, Tennessee. Her poetry chapbook, *Twisted Roots*, was published in 2011 by Finishing Line Press. Other poems have been published in *Kakalak Anthology of Carolina Poets*; the University of Maine's *Binnacle Poetry Journal*; *Maypop Journal*; *Glass: A Journal of Poetry*; *The Light of Ordinary Things* by Fearless Books; *Chantarelle's Notebook*; *Now & Then: The Appalachian Magazine* and *Still: Literature of the Mountain South*.

JUDITH L. DUVALL's poems and fiction have been published by Greyhound Books, Tellico Books, Kudzu Literary Anthology, and an upcoming edition of *Motif.* She attributes much of her success as a writer and poet to the support of fellow members of the Knoxville Writers' Guild, especially the Poetry Workshop group. After years of moving around the USA and other countries, she now lives, dreams, and writes near English Mountain and Douglas Lake in Jefferson County, Tennessee.

DEBRA DYLAN "'She's a poet. She didn't know it. And the wind, you can blow it,' 'cause I'm Ms. Debra Dylan. Yes, I legally changed my last name to match that of Bob Dylan. And yes, this bio is a hat tip to Syd Barrett—in case you didn't know it."

KESI GARCÍA is a Sevier County native and local high-school Spanish teacher. She graduated from the University of Tennessee with a B.A. in Spanish. Her short stories appeared in *Outscape: Writing on Fences and Frontiers* and *A Knoxville Christmas 2008.* Her toddler prefers Mommy dabbling in poetry more than constructing worlds in stories, as poetry allows more time for reading board books and rocking baby dolls.

MICHAEL GILL is a native East Tennessean, born in White Pine and raised in Knox County, a graduate of the University of Tennessee with a B. S. in Plant & Soil Science, and a former Peace Corps Volunteer in Lesotho, southern Africa. He is currently the *Alive After Five* Coordinator at the Knoxville Museum of Art, head honcho of Bluegill Productions, and writer of *Bluegill's Pond*, a Knoxville entertainment news e-letter.

CONNIE JORDAN GREEN writes and gardens on a farm in East Tennessee. She is the author of two novels for young people (*The War at Home* and *Emmy*) and two books of poetry (*Slow Children Playing* and *Regret Comes to Tea*). Her poetry has appeared in numerous journals and anthologies. Since 1978 she has written a newspaper column for *The Loudon County News Herald.* She and her husband have three grown children and seven grandchildren.

JUDY LEE GREEN is an award-winning writer and speaker whose spirit and roots reach deep into the Appalachian Mountains. Tennessee-bred and cornbread-fed, she has been published hundreds of times and received dozens of awards for her work. She shares life stories with others, teaching and enabling them to harvest their own memories and flex their memory muscles. She has been published in *Now and Then: The Appalachian Magazine, Passager, Christian Woman, The Rambler, New Southerner Magazine, The Village Pariah, New England Writers, Ultimate Christian Living,* various *Chicken Soup for the Soul* publications, and numerous anthologies. She lives in Murfreesboro, Tennessee.

BRIAN GRIFFIN holds an M.F.A. in Creative Writing from the University of Virginia. His fiction, poetry and essays have been widely published in literary journals and anthologies, and his collection *Sparkman in the Sky and Other Stories* received the Mary McCarthy Prize for Short Fiction. He is a former Director of Religious Education at Tennessee Valley Unitarian Universalist Church.

MELANIE HARLESS became a freelance writer after her retirement as a school librarian in Oak Ridge in 2006. She began writing a column on regional travel for a local news-magazine in February 2008. In addition to travel writing, she writes creative nonfiction, poetry, and short stories. Melanie has been published in four anthologies and in various print and online magazines and newspapers. She serves on the board of the Tennessee Mountain Writers.

J.L. HENSLEY was born in the mountains of Appalachia. He earned his B.S. and M.S. from the University of Tennessee and founded the Half Dead Poets' Society of Zihuatanejo, MXA. He is a good husband, father, and grandfather who resides in Gatlinburg, Tennessee, at his mountain cabin, Sawbriar.

PATRICIA A. HOPE of Oak Ridge, Tennessee, has won awards in poetry, fiction, and nonfiction. Her work has appeared in numerous publications including poetry and photographs in the online literary journal *Maypop* and a short story in *Muscadine Lines.* Her work has been used in the poetry anthology *Rubber Side Down,* and appeared in *Mature Living, The Writer, Blue Ridge Country,* and many area newspapers. In 2010 she edited the poetry anthology *Remember September: Prompted Poetry.*

ELIZABETH HOWARD lives in Crossville, Tennessee. Her work has appeared in earlier Knoxville Writers' Guild publications: *All Around Us: Poems from the Valley* and *Low Explosions: Writings on the Body* (2006). Her work has also appeared in *Comstock Review, Big Muddy, Appalachian Heritage, Cold Mountain Review, Mobius, Poem, Motif, Now & Then, Slant,* and other journals.

LAUREN HUTCHINS, a single mother to eight-year-old daughter Chloe and kitty cat Sneakers, is also a full-time student working towards a degree in education, along with being a part-time nanny and leader of Chloe's Brownie troop. In her free time, she enjoys girls' nights, road trips with Chloe, singing to the radio, writing poetry, and becoming absorbed in a good book or movie. "Sweet Sloppy Kisses" is her third published poem.

WILLIAM ISOM II is a native of East Tennessee, born and raised on the Hamblen County side of the Nolichucky River. He's a media justice worker, artist, cultural organizer and the father of two young men. Currently, he is one of the managers of The Neighborhood Center, a community space located in Knoxville's historic 4th & Gill Neighborhood.

CHRISTINE DANO JOHNSON's writing has recently been featured in *Seeing: The Everyday Magazine,* and *The Ends of the Earth* anthology. Her essay, "Tectonic Shift," won the 2010 Friends of the Knox County Library's Big Read essay contest. She is also the editor of *Far Away Literary Magazine,* an online and print literary and art journal. Christine composes poetry, fiction, and personal essays daily at http://silverfinofhope.wordpress.com.

GARY R. JOHNSON works as a Director of Photography in the television industry. He resides in West Knoxville, having returned to East Tennessee after living in Southeastern Alaska. His photographs have been seen in national touring exhibitions, on book covers, and in literary and art journals. More of his work can be found at http://www.grjohnsonphotography.com/.

LARRY JOHNSON, born in 1945 in Natchez, Mississippi, is the author of *Veins* (David Robert Books, 2009) and has published poems in many magazines. He received the second MFA in Poetry ever given at the University of Arkansas and later lived in Knoxville from 1973 to 1982, attending UT as a PhD student. In the fall of 2006 he read a selection of his poems at the Library of Congress. He lives in Raleigh, NC, and teaches at Wake Technical Community College.

SHANNON JONES, 22, is an original and dedicated artist, born and raised in Paint Rock, Tennessee. She studies multiple types of media, but is most passionate about painting and drawing. She creates a wide variety of subjects and has recently developed a technique she calls "Sling-Printing," which was inspired by her studies of Jackson Pollock. Shannon currently works as a graphic designer, creating billboards and various print media.

MARILYN KALLET is the author of 15 books, including *Packing Light: New and Selected Poems*; *The Big Game*, translated from Benjamin Péret's *Le grand jeu*; and *Last Love Poems of Paul Eluard*, all from Black Widow Press. She directs the Creative Writing Program at the University of Tennessee, where she is Professor of English. She also teaches poetry workshops for the Virginia Center for the Creative Arts, in Auvillar, France.

DONN KING is Associate Professor of Speech and Journalism at Pellissippi State Community College in Knoxville, Tennessee, as well as a writer and computer geek. His background includes newspaper, radio, small magazines and other publications, including co-authoring a textbook.

DAMARIS VICTORIA KRYAH studied for twenty-four years with a Zen Master: a gray-and-white Persian cat named Squeaky. "She helped me perfect the art of looking, which I have spent most of my life doing. I photograph and write to explore what can't be said. My life is art. My heart has been my most sensitive eye and I have used it to explore the myriad of impressions that come my way every day."

JUDY LOEST was born in Snowflake, Virginia and earned her Master's degree in English from the University of Tennessee in 1998. Her poetry has appeared in *Now & Then, Cortland Review, storySouth*, Poetry Society of America's *Poetry in*

Motion program, and Ted Kooser's "American Life in Poetry" newspaper column. She edited *Knoxville Bound*; her poetry chapbook, *After Appalachia*, was published in 2007.

LAURA LONG's artistic endeavors include creative journalism, fiction writing, painting, and photography. Her work has appeared in *The Nashville Scene* and *Starlog* magazine, *The Late Late Show* (web zine), and in KWG's 2008 anthology, *Outscape: Writings on Fences and Frontiers*. She is currently the publisher of CelebrateKnoxville.com.

DALE MACKEY is a poet, playwright, actor and amateur ukulele player who spends her days working at Community Television of Knoxville. She currently serves on the board of the Knoxville Writers' Guild, is a member of Knoxville's Actors' Co-op and is the co-founder of Artistic License, an organization dedicated to facilitating creative collaborations in and around Knoxville (www.artisticlicense project.com). You can learn more about her at www.DaleMackey.com

JOAN PARKER MacREYNOLDS was born and raised in Knoxville, TN. "I have an MS degree in Human Nutrition from the University of TN, worked at the University of Colorado Medical Center; taught school in Atlanta and France for several years; sailed for a year from Los Angeles to St Petersburg, FL in a Columbia 36 with my late husband; traveled extensively and spent thirty years in the art industry. I live in Knoxville with my husband Carmen and cat Lily."

JOHN C. MANNONE is the poetry editor for *Silver Blade* and the assistant poetry editor for *Abyss & Apex Magazine of Speculative Fiction*. Nominated three times for the Pushcart and once for the Rhysling Poetry Award, he has poems appearing in *The Pedestal, Glass, Lucid Rhythms, Prime Mincer, Aethlon, Mobius, Apollo's Lyre,* and *Wordgathering*. Visit *The Art of Poetry*: http://jcmannone.wordpress.com. He teaches college physics at Bryan College and serves as a NASA/JPL Solar System Ambassador.

LINDA PARSONS MARION's third and most recent poetry collection, *Bound*, chronicles the work and fabric of five generations of a Tennessee family, bound on journeys together and apart. She is published widely and is an editor at the University of Tennessee in Knoxville.

CYNTHIA MARKERT has been a painter for 35 years who has a love for photography. "I have a series called 'my knoxville' and 'my maplehurst'; this anthology's cover photo is of Knoxville's Henley Street Bridge in one stage of its deconstruction and rebuilding. I photograph it nearly every day and hope to do a show about this process when it nears completion, as I live within sight and sound of it!"

MARGO MILLER is a poet, avid crafter, cultural activist, creative expressionist, and documentarian who was born and raised in East Tennessee. She believes art is a powerful tool for organizing and uniting communities, not to mention an essential part of life. Whether it's in a poem or a photo, Miller aims to capture and share the simple sound-bites and snapshots that add the spice of life we may need reminding of every now and then.

ELI MITCHELL is a 70-year-old upstart writer who has "practiced" psychotherapy for 37 years. Colluding with co-author John Hoover, he shamelessly self-published *The Elders Speak: Two Psychologists Share Their Lifetimes of Experience* (2010). Eli's next expository venture is to illuminate his heritage starting with a (many-times-great) grandfather, the Reverend Samuel Thomas. This Anglican missionary was sent (1702) to South Carolina by—get this—the "Society for the Propagation of the Gospel in Foreign Parts." Stay tuned.

JO ANN PANTANIZOPOULOS has made many journeys, both geographical and cultural, in her life. A sign that hangs over her washing machine reads: "I wasn't born in Tennessee, but I got here as fast as I could." After being raised in Roswell, New Mexico, living in Greece and Switzerland for eight years and acquiring two new languages, she eventually landed in Knoxville. She has published translations of Greek lullabies, articles on young adult literature, and personal essays and poetry in many Guild anthologies as well as *Motif: Writing by Ear: An Anthology of Writings about Music.*

CHRISTINE PARKHURST, a teacher and writer, lives in Farragut, Tennessee, with her husband George and their two dogs, Juno and Simon.

CHARLOTTE PENCE recently earned her Ph.D. in English, with a concentration in creative writing, from UT. She is the author of two award-winning poetry chapbooks, *Weaves a Clear Night* (Flying Trout Press) and *The Braches, the Axe, the Missing* (forthcoming from Black Lawrence Press, May 2012). She is also editor of an essay collection slated to be published in January 2012 by University Press of Mississippi titled *The Poetics of American Song Lyrics.*

DICK PENNER grew up in the bizarro environs of Dallas, where he co-wrote one-half of the Rockabilly song, "Ooby Dooby," recorded by Roy Orbison, Credence Clearwater Revival, and scores of others. Many believe this to be Penner's Lifetime Achievement, at age twenty-one. Published two scholarly books, edited and wrote critical essays for his anthology, *Fiction of the Absurd* (1980), his own favorite, while he was a Professor of English at U.T.K., 1965-99. His photographs have won awards in regional and state competitions. Penner is very proud of his two sons, Richard and Greg. Currently, he resides in N.E. Knoxville in relative obscurity, from which he occasionally emerges, posing as an elderly, rakish roué.

JAN PERKINS is a native of East Tennessee who now lives in a log cabin in the Smoky Mountains where she keeps bees and cares for her many pets. After studying psychology at the University of Tennessee, she worked in the mental health field for several years and then owned and managed a medical transcription business for a number of years. She writes fiction, articles, and occasionally poetry.

HECTOR QIRKO lived off and on in Knoxville for over 30 years. He played and recorded music with the HQ Band, RB Morris, Lonesome Coyotes, and Balboa, was a half-time Lecturer and Adjunct Assistant Professor of Anthropology at the University of Tennessee, and worked as a consultant in organizational culture and diversity for the Tennessee Valley Authority and other organizations. He is presently Assistant Professor of Anthropology at the College of Charleston in Charleston, South Carolina.

JOE RECTOR is a columnist and novelist. He released his first novel, *Baseball Boys*, in 2011(Amazon.com) and is working on his second one for publication in 2012. His work also has appeared in several *Chicken Soup for the Soul* books, the KWG anthology *Low Explosions*, and various magazines. He has written for three Knoxville papers after working for 30 years as a high-school English teacher. Contact him at joerector@comcast.net.

RICHARD P. REMINE's photographs, and an occasional poem, have been included in three previous Knoxville Writer's Guild anthologies, as well as the two volumes of KWG's *A Knoxville Christmas*. A native of Knoxville, Richard likes to travel the landscape of back roads and blue highways, especially in East Tennessee, where he always expects to discover elements in nature, notably human nature, ranging from the ridiculous to the sublime. He is never disappointed.

JACK RENTFRO has written for numerous local publications since graduating from the University of Tennessee's journalism school. His work has been in six consecutive KWG anthologies and won various writing awards. He is the author and editor of *Cumberland Avenue Revisited: Four Decades of Music from Knoxville, Tennessee*, an anthology combining his interests in history, journalism and music. Rentfro currently writes for *Knoxville Magazine* and performs with his musical Spoken Word group, the Apocalypso Quartet.

JANE SASSER's poetry has appeared in *The Atlanta Review*, the *North American Review*, the *Journal of the American Medical Association*, *The Lullwater Review*, *Appalachian Heritage*, and various other publications as well as two chapbooks, *Recollecting the Snow* and *Itinerant*. She is a high-school English teacher in Oak Ridge, Tennessee. She shares her life with her husband George, greyhounds Emma and Dixie, and an ever-shifting pack of rescue foster greyhounds.

WILLA SCHNEBERG's three poetry collections are: *Box Poems, Storytelling In Cambodia,* and *In The Margins of The World,* which received the Oregon Book Award in Poetry. Her poems have appeared in *American Poetry Review, Salmagundi, Women's Review of Books* and *Poet Lore,* and other journals. Willa lived in Knoxville from 1981-1983, attended U.T., where she earned an MSSW degree. She worked in the 1982 World's Fair's Folk Life Center. Her website: threewayconversation.org.

PAMELA SCHOENEWALDT's historical novel of immigration, *When We Were Strangers* (HarperCollins, 2011) was a Barnes & Noble Great New Writers Discovery Selection. Her award-winning short stories have been published in England, France, Italy and the U.S.; a one-act play in Italian was produced in Naples. She has taught writing at the University of Tennessee and University of Maryland, European Division, and was Writer in Residence at UT. She is working on her second novel.

LUCY SIEGER lives in Knoxville, Tennessee, with her husband Mark and their two dogs, Daisy and Jasper. She believes our commonalities far outweigh our differences, and enjoys connecting her own idiosyncrasies to the broader human experience through personal essays and the occasional poem.

AMY STAFFARONI spent the past year in Knoxville as a CAC AmeriCorps volunteer at Tribe One. She is currently living in Brooklyn NYC, working as an apprentice at the Edible Schoolyard teaching students and parents about gardening and the importance of being connected to the food we eat.

D. ANTWAN STEWART is the author of two chapbooks: *The Terribly Beautiful* and *Sotto Voce*. His poems have also appeared in *Callaloo, Meridian, Poet Lore, Seattle Review* and the *Southern Poetry Anthology, Vol. III: Contemporary Appalachia*. He has received fellowships from the Bucknell Seminar for Younger Poets and the Michener Center for Writers, where he earned an MFA in poetry.

RONNIE JAMES VADALA resides in the Great Smoky Mountains of East Tennessee. In 1971, Ron recorded his first vinyl recording in New York City, of 2 original songs, with his band "The Sound Project" at Maino Music Studios. His primary interest is songwriting, and he has copyrights for over 50 songs of all genres. His CDs, produced under the JameSongs label, include: "Salem Station Boulevard," "The Sky is Blue," and "RestlesSoul." His music was broadcast on New York's CUNY radio in Brooklyn, as well as on live & pre-recorded radio broadcasts in Tennessee, in Knoxville (WDVX-FM), and in Newport (WLIK-AM).

PENNY L. WALLACE has been an avid photo bug for over 35 years. "My areas of interest cover various subject matter from military funerals to humorous dogs in sunglasses. Regardless of the subject matter, I try to capture the subject's raw emotion and strive for photos that don't require computer enhancement. I provide photography services for Second Harvest Food Bank and Knox Area Rescue Mission."

JANIE DEMPSEY WATTS writes both fiction and nonfiction. Her stories have been published in *Southern Women's Review* and *Blue Crow Magazine* and honored by the Pirate's Alley William Faulkner Creative Writing Competition as finalist and semi-finalist. Her nonfiction has been published in the *Christian Science Monitor, The Ultimate Gardener,* and the *Chicken Soup for the Soul* books. She writes for *Georgia Backroads* and her column appears in *Catoosa Life Magazine.* Please visit her at http://www.janiewatts.com/.

KIM R. WEST is a freelance photographer, writer of fiction, and environmental activist as well as a multi-talented technical writer, publications designer, and graphic artist. She has completed several years of undergraduate study in computer sciences, programming, and business administration; earned her Publications Specialist Certification at George Washington University; and is currently studying for her Certified Internet Webmaster national certification at the Tennessee Technology Center.

MELYNDA MOORE WHETSEL: "A retired art teacher who left the classroom to be an artist, I have yet to find the dedication to live in the studio. My studio is in the garden. Only when the rain pours or the temperatures freeze will I be found 'making art.' Even then the images do not venture far from flora and architecture, and the essence of the work is design— shape, color, texture dominate the space, command attention; contrast, balance, rhythm cause the eye to dance, dig, retreat, linger. The intention, like that of any beautiful garden, is to evoke a sense of time and place, and to cause the heart to ponder. My artwork has won frequent awards and is found in both public (Tennessee State Museum) and private collections."

ARTRESS BETHANY WHITE currently serves as Assistant Professor of English at Carson-Newman College. She earned her Master's degree in Creative Writing from New York University and a PhD in English from the University of Kentucky. Her poems have recently appeared in *Appalachian Journal* and *MELUS*, and are forthcoming in *Harvard Review*.

MARIANNE WORTHINGTON is a native of Knoxville, Tennessee. She is poetry editor for *Now & Then: The Appalachian Magazine* and co-founder and poetry editor of the online literary journal *Still: The Journal*. She is editor of the *Motif* Anthology Series from MotesBooks. She lives, writes and teaches in Williamsburg, Kentucky.

RAY ZIMMERMAN is the Executive Editor of *Southern Light: Twelve Contemporary Southern Poets*. He is a former president of the Chattanooga Writers Guild and won second place in the 2007 poetry contest of the Tennessee Writers Alliance. Ten days after coronary bypass surgery, he read his winning poem, "Glen Falls Trail," at the Southern Festival of Books, Legislative Plaza, Nashville. Ray was the subject of a feature article in *Blush* magazine.

Index of Contributors

Knoxville Writers' Guild

Board of Directors

Terry Shaw, President
Judith L. Duvall, Vice President
Margery Weber Bensey, Secretary
Martha Yarnell, Treasurer

Robert Cumming
Judy Lockhart DiGregorio
Jeff Gordon
Cathy Kodra
Dale Mackey
Sean McDougle
Kali Meister
Bonny Millard
Josh Robbins

Knoxville Writers' Guild

P.O. Box 10326

Knoxville, Tennessee 37939-0326

www.knoxvillewritersguild.org

CPSIA information can be obtained at www.ICGtesting.com
Printed in the USA
LVOW070004231111

256097LV00004B/4/P